Silent Treatment

By

Jackie Williams

Front Cover Photography

Natalie Williams

Silent Treatment

Copyright © 2011

Jackie Williams

All rights are reserved. This book may not be copied,
used or lent in whole or in part by any means
whatsoever without written consent from the author

This book is entirely a work of fiction.
All characters are products of
the authors imagination and any resemblance to actual
persons is entirely coincidental.

Silent Treatment

Chapter One

Harrow High School
April 2007

"What the hell..? For crying out loud Jen, I've had enough of this rubbish." Carrie muttered miserably and stepped back quickly as she surveyed the mess inside her locker. She obviously hadn't mislaid her key the week before.

Jealousy perhaps? Or maybe it was envy? She couldn't decide which as she picked out her history homework from amongst the sticky mess and shook off the acid pink silly string. Ribbons of goo clung limply across the front of the nearest folders and gradually dripped from the files onto the newly mopped corridor floor.

She was almost sorry that she was sure who was behind it all. She pressed her lips together, determined not to feel upset.

It was all so petty, hardly worth worrying about anyway. Jen was obviously still hurting but nothing was going to change how things had worked out. Carrie lifted the book up and shook it slightly harder.

The incidents began soon after she had been persuaded to attend an audition with her then best friend, Jennifer Crane. Jennifer had been desperate to attend but was been far too nervous to go by herself.

Carrie remembered thinking at the time that Jen was being ridiculous. If you wanted a career as a dancer, an audition to become part of the backing crew to a new boy band wasn't the best place to start if you couldn't even get up on a stage without your best friend holding your hand.

A sudden nasal sniff distracted her from her reverie.

"What the…Detention Miss Denton!" Carrie jumped back from her dripping locker as the ever vigilant school caretaker slid up beside her.

He drew in a deep breath.

"Befouling school property! You'll be lucky not to be suspended when I report this to the head." Mr. Evans looked down his long nose at her, hiding his glee badly and almost chuckling in triumph as he surveyed the mess dripping slowly to the floor.

Carrie tried desperately not to be distracted by the enormous amount of black hairs that tufted out of his quivering nostrils and attempted to explain.

"But I haven't done this Mr. Evans. My key went missing last week and now some idiot has sabotaged my locker. My stuff is ruined." She protested as she pointed to the sloppy mess that covered the inside of the tall grey box.

Mr. Evans sniffed loudly and Carrie watched in horrified fascination as the caretaker's nostrils flared even wider and the hairs in his nose wriggled in rhythm with his speech.

"Is this your locker or not?" He demanded loudly as he peered down his long nose at her.

She sighed and nodded stiffly but didn't speak. There was really no point in saying anything. He rattled on.

"Then I'm afraid this disgusting mess is your responsibility. I expect this lot to be cleaned up immediately and the floor too. I'm not employed to tidy up after the likes of you students. I expect to see you in detention after school on Thursday." He said it silkily, as though he were giving her a present, not a punishment, then he abruptly turned his back to her and stalked back off down the now deserted corridor.

Carrie wondered for a moment who a school caretaker was supposed to clean up after if it wasn't the school students, but then she heaved another great sigh as she swung back to her locker, silently cursing the day she had fallen out with Jennifer Crane...

She had only given in and gone to the audition because Jen had begged her. Carrie wasn't sure if it were her type of thing at all. She loved dancing but he had never really considered making a career out of it. She didn't see how you could. To her it was far more

7

important for the exercise and tone it gave to her body. She seriously thought she was too small and nowhere near attractive enough to be anyone's backing dancer. All the professionals she had ever seen appeared to be far more glamorous than she could ever hope to become.

But after both she and Jennifer had fought their way through the uncomfortably crowded London Underground, and when Carrie had looked at who else was attending the audition, she decided that she might as well enjoy the day and go for it after all. If nothing else at least she would be allowed to perform on a London stage for once in her life.

She had listened carefully when the choreographer explained exactly what the casting directors were looking for and had stood quietly waiting for her turn to impress.

Jennifer had immediately turned her back on Carrie and struck up a friendship with another beautiful, willowy young hopeful. She had spent the waiting hours completely ignoring Carrie, while gossiping about dancing to her new best friend.

Carrie kept herself almost hidden at the back of the crowd of hopeful dancers, practicing the given routine and stretching gently while trying to keep calm. And then, after what seemed an age, it was her turn.

The auditions were nearly over, almost seven hours after they had first arrived and the auditorium was practically empty, with only two or three young women waiting behind her.

There was a short pause in the proceedings as the girl before her was practically dragged from the stage by two burley men, while she shouted and screeched obscenities at the gawping producers when they didn't offer her a contract.

Carrie waited patiently until the fuss had died down. She felt so small she was almost embarrassed as she walked out onto the incredibly wide stage.

Two of the producers were talking between themselves, while the other only glanced briefly to look disinterestedly up and down her tiny frame.

Then he yawned loudly and looked down at his watch as though there really wasn't enough time for her to go on. He sighed deeply before he rolled his eyes and nodded curtly towards the sound man.

Carrie knew immediately that the three of them were completely bored with the day of auditions. Only a handful of hopefuls had won a contract. After seven hours they were barely concentrating at all and it was obvious that she wasn't what they were looking for, but she had been promised a chance to dance and she was determined to liven up the now stagnant atmosphere.

The music started.

Carrie exploded into the routine, pent up power and adrenalin surging through her body as she released the day's tension at last. She made every move bigger and better than she had been shown, more precise and seemingly effortlessly executed. She spun across the stage in her own interpretation of the given routine keeping in perfect time to the rhythm of the music, every muscle in her body stretched to its very limit.

The routine only lasted for two minutes, but she gave them two minutes of everything she had. She stopped dead on the exact last beat of the music and stood, perfectly balanced, in her finishing pose, breathing hard, the sweat already dripping from her body.

She had blinked her slate grey eyes slowly at the now completely silent producers and stood pulling in deep breaths, waiting for their dismissal, while her heart rate returned to somewhere near normal.

There was another moment's pause as something like electricity crackled through the air, then one of the producers, the one who had yawned earlier, leaned forwards.

He peered at her from over the top of his glasses, as though she was some kind of strange new, alien creature, and then he turned and raised his eyebrows at his two colleagues, who were staring up at her open mouthed. Neither of them looked back at him. The first one nodded, then the second. The yawner beckoned her forwards, handed her a piece of paper and said two only words.

"You're in."

She had taken the piece of paper with a trembling hand and looked down at it in surprise. For two or three seconds she couldn't see it clearly as the dripping perspiration blurred her vision, then as she brushed the sweat from her brow, she saw the word in bold print at the top. "Contract."

To Carrie's complete astonishment, she had been chosen as one of the twelve dancers to be featured in a promotional video with new boy band, Half Past Blue.

Jennifer, who had danced an hour before her had not been given a piece of paper. She stood in the wings watching Carrie staring at the paper, in bitter, silent resentment. She had scowled from the side of the stage as a young woman walked up to Carrie with an enormous smile and another sheet of paper. The casting assistant quickly took her aside and talked her through the rehearsal schedules. She finished by giving her the address of the filming studio and a consent form for her parents to sign.

Jennifer had treated Carrie to icy silence all the way home, and her friend had given her the glacial treatment ever since.

At first Carrie had felt terrible for her friend, apologizing at almost every opportunity, but after a few days Carrie realized that she had nothing to apologize for.

Jennifer had had her chance. It wouldn't have made any difference whether Carrie had stayed at home and Jennifer had gone to the audition on her own. Though Jennifer was a superb dancer, elegant and graceful, she was just not the type the producers were looking for this time round. She was only furious because Carrie had been given the part when she hadn't been looking for it at all.

But now she had been given the chance there was no way she was turning it down. Who would? Carrie tried to explain and reason with her but Jennifer had only glared spitefully and turned her back on her old best friend.

Carrie tried to ignore the hurt her friend was causing her but she didn't have time to dwell on it.

The hard work had begun almost immediately. There had been a whirlwind of rehearsals and manic racing from school to the dance studios, meetings with the band and getting to know the other eleven dancers before what seemed like hundreds of 'takes' at the film studio.

Carrie hadn't told another soul about it all. Only her family and Jennifer knew, but the silly bullying started almost immediately after the audition. Carrie decided not to say anything about it. She knew Jennifer was feeling hurt and resentful, and Carrie didn't want to make things any worse between them, but then Half Past Blue's first single had raced to the top of the charts.

Suddenly she was either the most popular, or the

most hated girl in the school.

At this precise moment in time, as she tried to avoid the silly string dripping onto her uniform, she was obviously the most hated.

Carrie glared at the retreating caretaker's back. She was convinced that he enjoyed handing out detentions to innocent victims. *How could he be so unjust? Some people loved power a little too much!* She was fed up with these childish pranks. She had tried to be positive and hoped that it would all die down. It was nothing too terrible, nothing that made her feel like crying, just stupid annoying stuff like the mess now in her locker.

The day she thought she had lost her locker key, she had returned to the changing room after her dance lesson, put her feet back in her shoes and then immediately wrenched them back out as her toes had dug into squished bits of jam doughnut. A few days before that someone with a great aim, had lobbed an enormous blob of freshly chewed chewing gum into her newly styled hair as she walked along a crowded corridor.

She gave up feeling sorry for herself and dropped her bag on the floor. She picked out the other ruined books, making a half-hearted attempt at shifting the sticky goo, then she stopped as she heard more footsteps echoing along the corridor. She glanced out from behind the locker door hoping it wasn't the headmaster coming to give her a dressing down too.

She breathed in deeply and rolled her eyes in horror as she saw who was striding towards her.

Great! As if her day could get any worse!

Daniel Lewis, the year thirteen heart throb was staring right at her, his sapphire blue eyes ice like in their scrutiny. She closed her eyes briefly and buried her head back in the locker. *Why couldn't she be looking cool and fabulous? Why did she have to have to have pink goo dripping from everywhere?*

At six feet six inches, Daniel was a giant. Taller than all the teachers, master of all sports and Captain of the school rugby team. Massive across the shoulders and slim at the waist, he was utterly gorgeous to look at. His dark hair, still damp from the shower, was clinging to his forehead after the latest rugby match and Carrie's heart fluttered madly as he approached her.

She was in love with him of course, all the girls were, and who could blame them with such a perfect specimen of eighteen year old manhood draped before their eyes every day, but Carrie didn't hold out any hopes. She knew she was a long way down the pecking order. She just wasn't in the "in crowd" enough to be considered worthy of being asked out by the likes of the, beyond gorgeous, Daniel Lewis.

Not that he had a girlfriend that she knew of. All of his spare time was taken up on the sports field, and even if he did attract a crowd of adoring female fans at every event he took part in, he didn't seem that impressed by any of them.

"What's going on Carrie?" His voice, soft but deep, wafted over her as he leaned past her shoulder and peered into the offending locker. His blue eyes widened as he surveyed the damage. "Don't let Evans see this mess. He'll go mad." Daniel stepped back quickly, avoiding the livid pink tendrils, as Carrie shook out another book. She wiped the strands of silly string with her fingers, but they clung tenaciously to the cover of the file. She gave the book a last desperate shake.

"It's too late, he's already given me detention and I think he's going to say something to the head. He said I could be suspended." Carrie sighed miserably as she slid the bedraggled book into her bag.

Daniel looked momentarily shocked and then he threw his head back and laughed loudly. It was a lovely sound, deep and husky.

"You twit! I don't think a foamed locker is going to get you suspended Carrie. Here, I'll give you a hand." He leaned over her, dwarfing her slender frame. Carrie could smell the wonderful aftershave he always splashed on after his rugby sessions, wafting from his

15

warm body. Daniel pulled a damp towel out of his kit bag and began wiping the inside of the locker. The foam smeared around the grey interior.

Carrie sighed as the mess spread even further, but she didn't have the heart to tell him that he was making it worse. She put her hand on his huge forearm.

"Thanks, but you don't have to do that Dan. You're going to ruin your towel and make yourself late home." She smiled gently up at him as she remembered how he had manfully helped her with the doughnut shoes too.

He had hooked his long finger around the jammy mess of one she while she had cleaned out the other, as she had hopped along in bare feet to her next class. And he had been there to oversee the cutting of her hair when the chewing gum had done its work.

He had given complicated instructions as he made one of the girls layer her hair above the offending grey blob instead of chopping it through straight. His coming to her aid was getting to be a bit of a habit.

Although Carrie was two years younger than Daniel, she didn't feel as overawed by him as some of the girls in school. She got on really well with him. He lived at the end of her street and they had known each other for years.

But it was only in the last six months that she had finally realized that she was in love with him. She kicked herself mentally for not knowing what the

16

strange skipping sensation in her heart had meant, every time she had seen him since she was about six years old.

It was hopeless of course. She knew that he only thought of her as a neighbour, the little girl from down the street, but she liked the fact that most days he waited for her at the end of the road so that he could walk to school with her. It didn't mean anything, she knew that, it was just that he'd always done it, even right back as far as primary school.

Daniel turned his head slightly and laughed grimly at her as he began scooping up more of the gloopy foam.

"Don't worry about it. This is only my old rugby towel. It gets a lot worse on it than this stuff, and I won't be missing much at home. I think I'd rather stay here and help you clear up this lot."

Carrie looked at him quizzically not sure whether he wanted her to ask why he wasn't particularly keen on going home. Curiosity got the better of her.

"Why?" She asked after a few seconds silence.

Daniel pulled a big dollop of foam out of the locker and looked around for somewhere to put it. Carrie pulled an old plastic sandwich bag from her pocket and he shook the foam inside.

He stood pulling bits of foam from his fingers, then he glanced down at her, his blue eyes suddenly very intense as his dark eyebrows descended into a straight line over them.

"It's not good at home at the moment. My parents aren't getting on. I think they'd get divorced if they could actually afford to split up. As it is they just spend the whole time arguing about who should live where. It's awful. I'd rather stay here."

Carrie balled up the lunch bag and tipped the rest of the books into her duffel. She'd clean off any remaining foam when she arrived home.

"Oh, Dan that's terrible! What are you going to do if they split up? I mean this is your last year here, I thought you wanted to go away to university, will their decision affect that?" Carrie was almost too scared to ask. She was going to miss him terribly just not seeing him at school. If he went away she would be heartbroken.

He leaned towards her and suddenly lifted one of his huge hands to her mass of dark hair. He pulled a couple of strands gently and then frowned.

"You have some of this stuff stuck in your hair. It's not as bad as the chewing gum but it won't come out by pulling. Well, not pulling gently at any rate. I'm just spreading it." He glanced down at her face as he pulled a little harder.

Carrie winced slightly as she noticed the thin line of stubble across his arching top lip, and a new bruise coming out along his cheekbone, from the latest rugby challenge. He lifted his other hand to cup her face for support and ran his tongue over his perfect white teeth as he concentrated on her hair.

His hand was surprisingly soft. Carrie resisted the urge to lean into his palm as she felt her heart rate pick up to an alarming rhythm. She took some deep, steadying breaths and moved her face away from his hand.

"Leave it Dan, I'll wash it out later." She didn't really want to stop him touching her but apart from beginning to feel as though her hair was being pulled from her scalp, she didn't think she would be able to resist throwing herself into his arms if she stood there much longer. She brushed his hand away and a shiver of pleasure ran down her spine as their fingers met momentarily. "Come on tell me, what are you going to do next year?"

Daniel looked down from his great height, frowning at his hand and turning it over, then he looked up again, his dark blue eyes suddenly sparkling at her.

"Don't laugh, but I'm trying to get into a sports college in the States. I've sent off the applications but I haven't had a response yet. If I get the right results in my 'A' levels I want to go to Atlanta, they have the best training there."

Carrie was horrified, her heart leapt in her chest and her stomach fell to the floor, but she kept her face and her voice as neutral as possible.

"America! Wow! That's ambitious. What will the rest of the world do without you? I mean, what will all the rest of the female half of the world do without you?" She nudged his arm playfully and cemented the smile onto her face, trying not to think of what she would do without him herself.

He smiled widely now, showing his perfectly straight, white teeth, obviously relieved that she wasn't falling about the floor laughing at him.

"If I can get there I'm not going to miss the chance. It's a three year course, so it's not to be taken on lightly, but I have to do something with my education. I'm a bit like you with the dancing. That's just short term stuff. The rugby isn't going to last me forever, we get too many injuries or are just too old by the time we're about thirty, so I want something that will get me somewhere in the future too. They run a fantastic sports therapy course alongside the training and that ties in nicely with something else I really want to do. The scholarships are few and far between, but you never know, I may get lucky." He bent down and picked up her bag, swinging the locker door shut with his huge shoulder and swiping his towel across the drip splattered floor. Then he stood straight again. "Have you told anyone about this bullying?"

The change of subject surprised her. She looked up at him and raised her eyebrows.

"What's the point? It'll stop when whoever it is

gets bored. It's such stupid stuff." She snorted at the thought of the jam doughnuts. They had been really fresh and incredibly jammy. Anyone half sensible would have eaten them, not stuffed them in her shoes. "I don't want to make a fuss about it...How do you know it's bullying anyway? It could just be someone out to have a laugh at my expense."

For the first time Daniel looked uncomfortable. He shifted his feet and glanced away from her. Eventually he mumbled.

"Well, apart from having to help you out every time it happens, somebody just said something. I mean it's obviously not accidental. I don't remember who told me, word just gets around. Do you know why they're doing it?"

Carrie shrugged and was about to dismiss it but then she spoke again.

"Do you know that some girls here get bullied just for being too pretty? But I don't think I have a problem there." She wrinkled up her nose. There was no danger of her being picked upon for being too attractive. While she knew that she wasn't ugly, her milk white skin was just a little too pale, her near black hair was almost too dark. Her eyes had no definite colour, changing from slate grey to hazel depending on the light, and her slightly overfull rose red lips made her features striking more than pretty. "I think it's to do with that dance video. I think someone's jealous. It's

21

probably my ex-best friend Jennifer Crane, who dragged me along to the audition but didn't get any further, while I did. I think she wanted me to turn the place down, but it wouldn't have made any difference, she would still know that I was given the part while she wasn't. I'm pretty sure it's her, but I can't prove anything."

Daniel handed her bag over, his face a picture of confusion.

"Jennifer Crane? You mean you don't know it's…" He paused and then took a deep breath before continuing. "Well, if she would stoop to doing something like that, just because she didn't make the grade, she's an idiot! I can't stand people like that. She'd do better to put her efforts into trying harder next time. My best friend Paul and I will be loyal to each other no matter what. He's hoping for a place in America too and I'd love for him to do well even if I didn't. I'll be cheering him on regardless. He's my best friend now and always will be, whatever happens in the future." He paused and frowned suddenly. "But I don't understand, what do you mean about not being pretty? I think you're pretty and the video was great too. At least you dancing girls look better than that sappy bunch of choir boys who sing badly. You should do another one without them distracting the viewers with their tuneless warbling." His tone was firm as he grinned down at her.

She laughed and felt her cheeks flush at his compliments.

"So you're a big fan of the band then?" She laughed again as he rolled his eyes meaningfully, and then she carried on. "They're all-right actually, really friendly and most people seem to enjoy their singing even if you don't. We're doing another video for them already. They were so pleased with the first one they wanted us for their follow up and maybe for their first live tour. It's really hard work though and what with my GCSE's I'm finding it difficult to fit everything in. I don't need this kind of hassle as well." She nodded back to the locker. "And now I'm going to miss Thursday evening's revision class too. Evans will just make me sit in his dingy office for a whole hour, doing nothing. I could get so much done in that time."

Daniel looked worried for a moment, then his face brightened.

"I'll see if I can have a word with him. I'm coming in early tomorrow for another training session. The season's nearly over but we have the biggest two games coming up and Simms wants us in every day this week. Evans is always about then. I've been giving his son some tips on training so perhaps he'll listen to me." He puffed out his huge chest and Carrie thought that she would definitely listen if he came and talked to her. His size could be very frightening if you didn't know what a nice guy he was. She giggled as she thought how the year sevens cowered and fell back whenever either Daniel or any of his huge friends were around.

They walked down the corridor together and Carrie suddenly noticed that there were two or three other enormous year thirteen's hovering at the school door. They were looking slightly impatient and she realized that they were part of the rugby team. They had obviously been waiting for Daniel.

For a moment she felt overwhelmed by the size of them all as they gathered around their team captain, talking about the match and slapping each other on their backs as they congratulated themselves on the latest win.

Carrie quietly ducked under their massive arms and managed to slip away from the group unnoticed. She walked quickly out of the school gates and headed off down the road but she soon heard running footsteps and was suddenly grabbed on the shoulder.

Daniel's huge hand stopped her in her tracks. He looked down at her, a slight frown on his face.

"Do you want me to walk you home in case anyone's hanging around for you?" His face was full of concern.

Carrie felt her cheeks blush a deep red. Although they always walked in to school together, on the way home it was more of a falling into step because they were going in the same direction, rather than a deliberate thing. This was the first time he had ever asked her if she wanted him there.

"No." Her voice was just a little too high pitched. "Thanks for the offer but I'll be fine. You stay with your mates. Nobody has ever done anything to me outside school." She swung her bag up onto her shoulder again and walked down the road, wondering why he had felt the need to ask her. It was nice of him, but she didn't have far to go and he would be walking that way himself. He was probably only a few yards behind her.

She chanced a look back over her shoulder and noticed the group was following her slowly. Daniel's friend Paul was looking right at her. He glanced away as he caught her eye, then he looked up at her and raised his eyebrows as he turned back to Daniel. He shook his head at something Daniel had said and then laughed loudly and thumped him playfully on the shoulder.

Daniel looked momentarily furious, almost dangerous and then he glanced back over to Carrie. She smiled at him and he smiled back and suddenly his scowl was gone and he was laughing with his mates again.

Carrie turned around and headed for home without looking back again. At the path near the park she heard them head off in different directions and then she heard giant feet pounding along behind her.

Daniel caught up within a few seconds.

"Hang on Carrie." He puffed up to her. "We can walk together now. Paul's gone to pick up his kid sister, but those other idiots are going to have a fag in the park. Why they feel they have to go to the park I have no idea." He looked back over his shoulder and frowned at the clouds of smoke appearing around his friends. "I wonder if I can ban it if they want to stay on the team?"

Carrie laughed.

"I'd like to see you try."

Daniel glared down at her.

"It's not funny Carrie. I hate smoking. It's a vile habit and I can't believe they'd mess around with their fitness like that. They're obviously not taking their rugby seriously. I think I'm going to drop them if they don't quit." His was frowning in obvious irritation. Then he looked at Carrie. "Just tell me you'll never smoke Carrie, promise me you won't."

There was an urgency in his tone that Carrie didn't understand. She looked up at him. Why was he so concerned if she smoked or not? She never would, she hated it as much as he did but why did it matter to him?

"Of course I won't smoke Dan. If I'm going to get anywhere with this dancing lark, there's no way I can let anything like smoking interfere with my health."

He breathed out a huge sigh of relief.

"Good, but it's such a disgusting habit, I'm not going to let you get away without promising me." They were standing at his gate, but he didn't make any move to go inside.

She held her hand over her heart and grinned.

"That's easy Dan. I promise you, most faithfully, cross my heart and hope to die, that I will never smoke. Is that good enough for you?" She smiled up at him, but he didn't return the smile. He nodded grimly, his face remaining very serious.

He moved a little nearer to her and lifted his hand to her hair. His touch was so gentle and she felt a thrill run all the way through her body. He had never touched her like this before.

And then the long strands fell from his hand.

"Don't forget to wash your hair. That stuff is difficult to get out if it dries too hard." His voice was husky and Carrie gulped as she caught another waft of his fabulous aftershave.

She lifted her own hand and touched the stiffening strands, feeling very stupid as she realized that he was only reminding her about the silly string. She had forgotten about it completely.

"No, I won't forget." She whispered and she dropped her eyes.

And then he stepped away from her.

"Bye Carrie, I'll see you in the morning. I'm

going in at eight but you could come in early too and get some of that revision done. I'll meet you again tomorrow night and let you know what Evans says about letting you off the detention." He turned and pushed through the gate and walked slowly to his front door.

Carrie moved immediately. She almost ran up the road. Her cheeks were flaming, her heart pounding in her chest. *He was worried about her health and he had touched her hair twice. That had to mean something surely! It can't have just been about the silly string! And he was going to wait for her tomorrow after school again too!* She shoved her key in the lock and charged through her front door, slamming it behind her and breathing heavily as she leaned against the cool wood.

"That you Carrie?" Her mother shouted her usual greeting from the kitchen.

Carrie sighed and caught her breath. *Who else did her mother think it would be*? There was no one else in the house until her dad came in later.

"Yes mum. I'm going up for a shower. I got some stuff in my hair in science." She yelled back.

Her mother's head suddenly appeared around the kitchen door and Carrie caught sight of her dipped eyebrows and curious frown.

"What sort of stuff? I've a good mind to come up to that school and complain."

Carrie fended her mother off, waving her hand across her face as she dismissed her reaction as unnecessary.

"It's nothing serious mum, it's just a bit sticky. Are you taking me to rehearsals later or do I have to get the bus?"

Diverted, her mother answered quickly.

"I can drive you tonight. Antonio only wants you for an hour. He's got some big producer chap coming down from central London so he can't be with the group for too long. I think they have managed to negotiate a tour for you lot. He sounded very excited."

Carrie stopped at the bottom of the stairs thinking about what Daniel had said earlier. His words suddenly seemed very important.

"I can't go trekking about the country now mum. I have to do my exams. I can't give them up for some tour, I need to get good qualifications for if this doesn't work out. I don't want to end up stacking shelves in the supermarket."

Her mother walked along the hall to her.

"I don't think it will come to that Carrie. You are bright enough to do anything you want, but I understand what you are saying. I think Antonio was talking about during the summer holidays. The band has been booked for some of the festivals, but I don't want you to worry about it until we know for sure, okay. Now go get that stuff out of your hair." She

29

peered at Carrie's head suspiciously. "It looks a vile colour. Whatever were you doing in class to make that kind of mess?"

Carrie took a couple of steps up the stairs to avoid her mother's curious eyes.

"Oh, it's just some chemical reaction. It was an experiment but it kind of blew up in my face and went everywhere. It's not dangerous or anything so there's nothing to worry about. Can you make me a sandwich before dance? I'm famished." She ran up the rest of the stairs as her mother nodded and went back to the kitchen.

Carrie threw her bag onto her bed and looked in the mirror. She rolled her eyes and groaned in misery. Her hair was a matted smear of pink at one side and she had been talking to the man of her dreams as though there was nothing unusual in that.

She moved to her bedroom window as she thought of Daniel Lewis again. If she stood on the right of the glass and squinted sideways, she could just see into Daniel's back garden.

She had only made the discovery one evening in September the year before when she had heard the weirdest thumping, grunting noises coming from outside.

She had been laying on her bed thinking that maybe someone was practicing wrestling, but when she had mentioned the odd noise later that evening, her dad had shaken his head in resignation. He had moaned over their dinner as the grunts had carried on into the night.

"It's that blasted kid up the road. You know, the huge one. I wish he would give up the rugby practice in the evenings. That training machine he uses is doing my head in, and the noises he makes! Sounds like a rutting elephant! He's built like a brick shit-house as it is. You wouldn't think he needs to build up any more. I'd complain if his whole family wasn't so blasted huge."

Carrie's mother had told her husband off for using unsuitable and bad language and Carrie had slipped away up to her bedroom just to see if she could see what her father had been talking about.

She had been surprised that any noise from Daniel's house would travel all the way up the street, but when she looked out of the window she realized, for the first time, that the road wasn't quite straight and the gardens curved into a long looping arc. The end of his back garden was nearer to hers than she had thought.

She had craned her neck against the window and, out of the corner of her eye, less than a hundred metres away, she had seen a blur of someone charging down a garden, and then a full throated growl could be heard as Daniel hit a big padded frame at the end. He pushed the frame back hard with his shoulder, keeping the pressure up for several seconds, before he backed off and strode down the garden, only to turn and repeat the whole process again.

Carrie had watched him night after night since.

Now she pressed her cheek against the cool glass and was rewarded for her uncomfortable position as Daniel stepped out of the back of his house, dressed in only shorts and a vest, rolling his massive shoulders before eyeing up his target.

He charged, with blinding speed, at the frame. But this time he didn't stop there. He stepped straight back and swung his fist at the padding, knocking it back on its springs. It bounced back towards him but, as quick as a flash, he caught it another hefty whack.

This time he let out a huge yell, but it wasn't his usual yell of satisfaction. It was a yell of pure frustration and anger, and as if to make sure about it, he stood away from the bag and roared furiously into the air.

Carrie stepped back from the window and rubbed her cold cheek. What on earth was he so angry for? He had seemed all right just before she had left him. Maybe his mum and dad were arguing again.

She picked a towel up from the floor, feeling guilty about leaving it there the night before, and took it to the bathroom. She put it over the heated rail to air and began to undress.

She stepped into the shower and lathered her hair quickly, pulling the bits of congealed foam from the strands, then she gave an involuntary shiver as the soap sloshed down her body. She tried not to think of Daniel's huge muscled body as he threw himself at the padded frame.

It was too difficult. She knew it was wrong to even think it, and it made her blush to the roots of her hair, but she wished that he was in the shower with her, washing the slippery soap from her hair and then wrapping the towel around her shoulders and drying her off.

Carrie shivered again as she stepped out of the cubicle and grabbed the now warm towel from the rail. She wrapped it around her body and rubbed hard. She didn't have any more time to waste dreaming of Daniel and his beautifully sculpted muscles. She had to be out dancing in less than half an hour.

She grabbed her trackies and a baggy t-shirt and lugged them on over her still damp skin, then she picked up her trainers and a clean towel and ran back out of her room and down the stairs.

Chapter Two

Harrow High School
July 2007

Carrie put down her pen and sighed in relief. She tucked a loose strand of dark hair behind her ear, leafed back through the paper checking all her answers, then sat back in her chair. She had done as much as was possible. The final exam was over.

She glanced around the hall and saw that several other students had slumped back in their chairs too. Only one or two were still scribbling furiously, heads bent over their work. She looked up at the clock just as the minute hand reached the hour. The invigilator cleared his throat.

"Pens down every one, thank you. Please remain seated and silent until all the papers have been collected."

Carrie put her pen in her pocket and glanced over at her ex-best friend Jennifer Crane, who was at the next door desk. Her gaze was met by an icy glare.

Things had become no better since the audition and now everyone knew about the summer tour with the band too.

It was all the fault of the performing arts head who, even though she had been asked not to mention it, had blurted it out at their leavers' awards ceremony and had gushed endlessly about how proud the school was of Carrie's superb achievements.

Carrie had rolled her eyes in despair and lowered her head into her shoulders as she tried not to be noticed by the other pupils.

But then the posters had been pasted up in town. The boy band, Half Past Blue, were playing a two day gig at Harrow's biggest public park and, right in the middle of the publicity photograph for the band, Carrie could be seen quite clearly. She was in the back-ground right behind the lead singer, hair flying, dancing like fury.

Carrie had tried to talk to Jennifer about it all again, but she still wouldn't listen and in the end Carrie gave up. If she couldn't get over it then that was her problem not Carrie's. All Carrie could think about was how much hard work it all involved. She came home every night, shattered from all the rehearsals. Every bone in her body ached, muscles screamed in pain and on top of that, her social life was completely down the pan, because most of her so called friends were green with envy and could barely speak to her for jealousy.

Carrie found the whole merry-go-round of emotions very wearing. While she loved and wanted to dance, it was now becoming a serious commitment and she would be giving up her summer holidays too. The band's tour was taking them around the whole country and the dancers had to follow them. In some ways she didn't want to go, but in others it was all so exciting.

She sometimes lay in bed at night, unable to sleep even though she was exhausted, with the whole mad affair running over and over through her head.

The hall started to empty. She stood up, shoved her chair beneath her desk and made for the door. It was only as she pushed through the swing doors of the sports hall that she noticed Jennifer and her friends. They were standing just to the side of the entrance, staring at her as she approached.

Carrie gave them a hopeful smile. Perhaps now that they were leaving school they could all be friends again.

But her heart sank as she reached them. Their hard expressions didn't change, and, as she made to walk through the gap, they suddenly all surged forwards together, smashing the heavy hall doors back towards her.

Carrie looked disbelievingly at Jennifer through the thick glass partition and noticed the sly, twisted smile spreading across her lips just as she tried to fend off the door. But she was too late and too hemmed in by other students to stop the collision from happening. Searing pain shot through her whole body and the next thing she knew, she was clutching at the top of her right arm almost unable to breathe through the agony.

Someone beside her was speaking, but her brain

couldn't register the words. Then one of the teachers was in front of her, steering her away from where she was crushed behind the door, and sitting her down on one of the now vacant exam chairs. Carrie thought she was going to pass out with the pain.

The next few moments were a blur of shouting and confusion and then suddenly Daniel Lewis was squatting in front of her, his beautiful blue eyes on a level with hers. His huge hands were on her shoulder, his heat travelling through her shirt to the agonized joint and taking some of the pain away. She shook her head, trying to clear her fuzzy brain.

Then Daniel was speaking to her, but she didn't know what he was saying. All she could see was his lips moving sensuously. She wriggled under his hand and winced as the pain brought her mind back into focus. She tried to concentrate on his words.

"Sit still Carrie. I think it's dislocated. You're going to have to go to the hospital. Come on, I just finished my last exam too so I'll take you to A & E. Paul will give us a lift in his car."

Carrie shook her head, ignoring the burning sensation in her neck, her eyes fearful as she realized exactly what he was saying. She gasped aloud as more pain shot through her shoulder and neck.

"No." She gasped frantically and then gulped for more air. "I can't go to A & E. If they strap me up I won't be allowed to dance. The tour starts in three weeks. It's all organized. I have to be in it. I can't let that cow beat me down any more. Please Dan, you know what to do. You took that course on injuries. Paul's shoulder came out during practice last year and you put it back in yourself. Just do what you did then and I'll be fine." Carrie gritted her teeth through the now throbbing pain.

Daniel's blue eyes pierced her as he sat back on his heels, his brows furrowed. He shook his head.

"No way Carrie. I can't do it. It was different with Paul. He's a bloke for a start and built to take pain like that, you're not. You're so small and fragile I could make things worse and then you might never get full strength back in it. That would ruin your chances of a dancing career forever. I can't take the risk."

Tears began to run down her face. She blinked them away furiously and gritted her teeth determinedly.

"Please Dan. Don't take me to the hospital. If you can put it back in place, I can rest it for the next couple of weeks. Paul was playing right after you did his, I saw him." She was begging him quietly, not wanting the hovering teacher to hear her words. "Just give it a try, I promise you can take me to the hospital if you can't get it back in first time, okay. Go on Dan, please, just one try." She bargained, her eyes never leaving his.

Daniel hesitated and then shook his head again. He looked as if he were about to be sick.

"It's going to be too painful. Carrie, I don't want to hurt you. Please don't make me."

Carrie took a deep breath and glared at him as she spoke with a voice of steel.

"Do it Daniel. I'm not nearly as fragile as you seem to think. I can take a bit of pain. Can't you see, if you don't try for me, then Jennifer Crane wins..." She paused as she watched his expression harden. "Do it now Daniel." She pressed her lips tightly together and set her jaw as she stared hard at him.

He stared back, hesitating for just one more moment before his eyes became even more intense, and then he nodded firmly. She closed her eyes as he pushed her hair back behind her neck and scrutinized her shoulder carefully, touching her lightly as he looked. Then he moved his hands a fraction, feeling around her shoulder joint, pressing with a gentle pressure on her skin. Then he grasped her arm more firmly between his palms.

"Look at me Carrie. Open your eyes and look right at me." He breathed quietly. She lifted her dark lashes and gasped. His gaze was burning into hers as his grip tightened and Carrie gazed right back at him as she clamped her teeth together.

There was a sudden sickening crunch echoing around the hall. Carrie didn't understand what the noise was for a second, and then a wall of agony slammed into her. She opened her mouth to scream, but nothing came out and then the room began to spin as she fell forwards into Daniel's outstretched arms, her head slamming into the rock hard wall of his chest.

The next second she was being lifted from the chair. Daniel swept her up into his arms and fended off with a look the teacher who came rushing up, demanding to know what he'd done.

Daniel's extreme height and confident manner had the teacher backing off seconds later.

"No, don't worry, she's fine. Just a bit faint. I'm a qualified first-aider. She's my neighbour so I can take her home. Her mum's there. She'll be better off with her family." The teacher looked relieved that he wasn't going to be held up and the small crowd that had gathered around them parted as Daniel carried her from the hall.

He strode out into the corridor, Carrie's head flopping against his shoulder, his huge arms cradling her gently. Daniel looked around the corridor frantically. He lifted his chin as he spotted his friend.

"Hey, Paul! Over here! Get your car out the front! We need to take Carrie home now!" He yelled over the crowd to his best friend. Paul looked surprised for a moment and then noticed Carrie's wilting form. He shoved through the curious crowd.

"What the hell happened?" Paul stood astonished for a second. He fell into step beside his best friend as they moved away from the staring pupils and walked down the corridor.

Daniel looked very worried. He bit his lip to stop the concern coming out in his voice.

"I just shoved her shoulder back into place. Some bunch of idiots slammed the fire doors on her as she came out of the hall and knocked it right out. I was just coming out of my last exam and saw the whole thing. They did it on purpose Paul." He sounded appalled.

Paul narrowed his eyes and winced as he shoved ahead, clearing the way to the doors.

"Bastards!" He growled with conviction. "Have they any idea what an injury like that can do? They need their bloody necks wringing. And she let you put it back? Shit, that's gonna hurt man. Damn near killed me when you did mine." He winced at the memory and glanced down at Carrie again. "You think she's okay? She looks pretty pale."

Daniel gazed down at Carrie, an almost bewildered look covering his face.

"She's always pale Paul. I don't think she looks any paler than normal. I think she's just gone faint from the pain. At least I'm hoping that's what it is. It went back in okay, made a horrible crunch, but then it slipped right back into the socket, didn't even feel like anything tore. I just want to get her out of here so I can check it out properly without half the school as an audience." Daniel looked down at Carrie's paler than

41

pale face.

Paul strode out in front of Daniel, driving a path through the crowds of curious students who had just finished their exams.

"I'll get the car. You need to sign her out?" He called over his shoulder as he began to jog along the corridor.

Daniel shook his head.

"Don't think so. That was her last exam so I think we can just leave. I'll meet you at the gate."

Carrie could hear them talking above her, but she felt as though she wasn't really there. She wasn't in pain any longer, but there was a strange numbness down one side of her neck. She tried to twist her head, but Daniel clamped his hand hard against the side of her face and pressed her into his iron chest. He glanced down and gave a grim smile.

"No, don't move until I can take a proper look at you. We're going to take you back to mine. If there's any problem at all we can take you on to the hospital from there."

Carrie found her voice at last.

"Why your place Dan? Why not take me home? My mum will be there." She sounded horribly weak and feeble.

Daniel raised his eyebrows as he glanced down at her again.

"I thought the whole point of me putting you

back together was so that no one found out about it. Your mum will have you out of that dance group in a flash if she knows what happened. She'd probably be right to do it too. God Carrie, I feel awful. I shouldn't have done it." His guilt ridden voice was agonized and he clutched her closer to him.

Carrie struggled feebly in his arms, wanting to prove that she was fine. She didn't want him to feel bad about what he had done, but she gave up almost immediately as she realized that her efforts were no match for his bulging muscles. She kept her voice steady as she spoke.

"I'll be fine. I can feel that it's okay. It's just a bit numb now. It was only the shock that made me faint. I didn't think it was going to hurt that much."

Carrie felt the rumble shudder through his chest as Daniel groaned.

"Numb? Oh no, I don't think it should be numb. God! I wish I had done the advanced course as well now." He sounded exasperated with himself.

They reached the car. Paul was waiting with the back door open. Daniel ducked his head and slid inside with Carrie still in his arms. He reached for the seatbelt and clipped it in around them both. Paul put the car in gear and took off slowly up the road.

Paul leapt out of the car as soon as they drew up to Daniel's house. He flung open the car door and took Carrie from Daniel's arms. She protested loudly that a shoulder injury didn't affect her walking ability, but they both ignored her and didn't put her down until they reached Daniel's front room. He shouldered his way inside and pushed open the door to the lounge. Paul moved forwards quickly, laid her gently on the couch and then stood back as Daniel knelt down in front of her.

Carrie immediately tried to sit upright, but as she put her hand down to push against the fabric of the settee, the shooting pain in her shoulder brought the nausea back to the surface. She leaned forwards and breathed deeply, holding back the vomit that rose into her throat.

"Give it a while. Don't put any pressure on it for a moment and the pain will go quicker." Paul spoke over Daniel's shoulder. "When Dan put mine back in last year, I actually thought he'd killed me, felt like he'd torn my arm off. It was numb for ages afterwards, and I felt as sick as a dog. Seemed like hours before I could even think of moving it, but really, after just a few minutes it was a bit better."

Daniel gave Paul a furious, accusing glare.

"You didn't say it hurt that much, you just walked off like it was fine right away. You were rolling it round like it was okay."

Paul gave a great laugh and slapped his friend on the back.

"Huh! That was for your benefit mate, you

know, just so you didn't feel too bad. I actually thought I was going to die from the pain. I only didn't say anything because I couldn't unclamp my jaws. If I had done I would have cried." Paul pulled a face as he remembered the agony.

Daniel glared at Paul, amazed at his confession.

"What real tears? Christ Paul! You should have told me. I would never have made Carrie suffer like this if I'd known it was that bad."

Paul shrugged dismissively.

"Just as well I didn't let on then. Carrie would have been up at the hospital and out of the dance team before she knew it. You can't let that happen without a bit of a fight." He looked back down at her. "As it is, there's no way you're going to be doing anything much with it for a day or two. Can you get out of any rehearsals?"

Carrie gave a small nod, anticipating pain. She winced as she was suitably rewarded.

"Probably. But maybe I can pretend I have a stomach bug or something. They won't want me around if they think I could spread an infection. Antonio makes us take a full twenty-four hours off after the last time we're ill, forty eight if we've actually been sick, just so that none of the rest of us catch anything. That will get me to Friday and then we've a two day rest break this weekend anyway."

Daniel turned to Paul, his tone like acid.

"Four days then. Was that long enough for you? And for God's sake tell me the truth this time."

Paul nodded. He was serious now.

"It'll be moving by then, but it'll still hurt like fu..," He cleared his throat noisily. "You know what I mean, but don't forget, I wasn't doing any wild arm movements anyway. If you remember I stayed well out of trouble for a couple of games…" He looked at Carrie. "Can you fake it in dance practice?" He squatted down beside Dan.

Carrie shook her head gently.

"Not a chance. Antonio goes mad if we don't put everything into it. He'll notice in a heartbeat if I'm holding back. The best I can get away with is if I said I slept on it funny and it's a bit stiff, but if I'm not okay in a couple of days, he'll have me at the physiotherapist's and she'll know what's wrong with it in a second." She looked at them both glumly. "This is going to be hard to pull off."

Daniel nodded, swivelled around and sat on the settee beside her. His thigh was just skimming her leg.

"Do you have to go into school for anything over the next couple of days?"

Carrie turned to him, wincing as the pain caught her off guard again.

"Ouch! No, that was my last exam, so I've officially left school now. I only have to go in to clear my locker and then I can be signed off for the summer."

"Paul will do your locker, won't you?" Daniel looked up at his friend who nodded immediately.

"Whatever you need pal." He answered firmly. "I have to go in anyway. My last geography exam is tomorrow, I can do it then."

Daniel turned to Carrie again.

"I'm finished with all mine. Took my last math's exam today, but maybe I can go in and have your end of year slip signed. If you can get away from your mum tomorrow you can come over here when I'm back and we can start on the physio straight away. I've been taking a course for the last year. Obviously I'm not qualified yet but I know the basics for shoulder injuries. What they did to you was a bit like being slammed by a defender. It'll be good practice for me anyway."

Carrie almost shrugged, but stopped herself in time

"I don't know how I'm going to get out of the house if I've told her I've got a stomach bug. I'll have to say something about wanting some fresh air, that might do it."

Paul stood up and rubbed the feeling back into his thighs. He looked at his watch.

"Well, if we're all okay here, I've gotta go man. I pick up my kid sister from drama club about now. She'll be a pain in the butt if I'm late." He gave a brief glance at Carrie. "You sure you don't want to go to the hospital? It's on the way to my sister's school."

Carrie shook her head automatically and then grinned as she realized her shoulder didn't hurt quite so badly.

"No, it's fine, I'm sure. I can feel it's getting better already. I'll go home in a while and have a good hot soak in the bath. I'll tell mum I feel a bit light headed after the exams. She'll fall for that. Then a bit later I'll go to bed and pretend I'm sick in the night. With a bit of luck, if I time it right, I can be ill for more than the two days, then I can get a third day off after. Another day resting will probably make a difference."

Daniel smiled at her, obviously relieved that she could move her head more now.

"Well Carrie Denton! I didn't know you could be quite so devious."

Carrie raised her eyebrows and felt her cheeks begin to flush.

Paul rolled his eyes at her and turned to leave.

"I'll see you later Dan, and if you leave your locker key with him Carrie, I'll pick up your stuff tomorrow. Maybe I'll see you back here, if you've got away with telling a few fibs."

Carrie smiled at him.

"Yeah maybe, and thanks for the lift Paul. See you tomorrow."

They stayed silent until they heard the door slam

and then Daniel turned to Carrie again.

"You sure about the hospital? I can get you there if you need to go. I passed my test earlier this year and I can borrow mum's car."

"Honestly, I'm fine, look." She lifted her shoulder tentatively. It hurt, but it wasn't unbearable. Daniel put his hand on the joint and pressed his fingers lightly around her whole shoulder, moving it gently as he checked to see that she had full movement. Then he laid the flat of his hand on her shoulder blade and began to massage it slowly.

Carrie sat up very straight. Her shoulder had been burning with pain, but now her whole body felt as though it were on fire. His hands were firm but gentle as they massaged deep into her muscle and then he moved one hand to the back of her neck. His hand was so large she could tell he could almost encircle her whole neck with it, but he kept his fingertips on the muscles just beneath her head and rolled them with a gentle pressure.

The sensations were so intoxicating that an involuntary groan left her lips and Daniel moved his hands away from her quickly.

"Sorry!" He exclaimed. "I didn't mean to hurt you." His voice was very near her ear and she was more than relieved that he had thought her in pain and not enjoying the experience of him touching her so much that she had lost control of her voice box.

"Perhaps I'd better not do any more to it today." He added quietly.

She couldn't help herself as she spoke.

"No, carry on for a bit, it's really soothing. I don't want to look all stiff when I go home. Mum has eyes like a hawk and will spot it straight off." Her heart thumped erratically as she spoke, but he put his hands back on her and began moving them rhythmically again.

She tried rolling her head from side to side as he massaged and then turned it either way. As she turned to the right she caught Daniel looking directly at her. She stopped twisting her head and stared back at him.

He seemed to hesitate for a moment, but then spoke quickly as he massaged some more.

"I won my scholarship place in America." He didn't stop speaking as Carrie felt her face crumple. "As long as I get 2 A's out of my four subjects and pass the other two with at least a B, I can start early September. I'm pretty sure I've done enough for that. It's going to be great 'cos Paul was awarded a place too. I just need to get my airfare together. I'm working Saturday and Sunday nights at the garage to help pay for it."

Carrie tried to fix her expression into one of delight. She didn't think, by the way her cheeks contracted violently, that it could look very convincing.

"That's fantastic. When did you hear?" She

gulped and had to stop speaking or she would have cried.

Daniel sat a little straighter.

"I only received the confirmation yesterday. I was worried for Paul. His parents are well off and he doesn't qualify for the full scholarship, but they've said they'll pay the difference for his first year. Hopefully he can get a decent job and earn enough while he's there to cover the rest of the course. I'm going to have to work too, but at least I'll only have to cover living expenses. We'll probably end up sharing somewhere and divvying up the money." Daniel didn't sound as enthusiastic as Carrie thought he should. He wasn't smiling at all.

She frowned up at him.

"Is something wrong Daniel? You don't sound very happy about it. Don't you want to go?" She knew her voice was trembling with emotion but there was nothing she could do about it. She felt her eyes begin to well up with tears and she blinked them back furiously, determined not to cry.

Daniel looked down and dropped his hands into his lap.

"I thought I wanted to go more than anything in the world, up until a few months ago. I still want to go really, but there's a complication that's come up big time, and I don't know how I can get around it." His tone was more than despondent.

Carrie felt as though her mouth would never work again, but she forced the words out from between her clamped jaws.

"What complication?"

Daniel lifted his blue eyes to hers again and Carrie suddenly felt very hot under his burning gaze.

"Don't you know? Can't you guess Carrie." He ran his fingers through his hair in obvious frustration. "The complication is you. I don't want to go and leave you. Not now." He sounded more than miserable.

For a moment she couldn't think what he meant. She was barely over the shock of him telling her that he was leaving England.

"Me? You don't have to worry about me. My shoulder will be fine by then." Her heart was banging in her chest, threatening to explode through her school shirt.

He suddenly laughed at her and then grabbed her hands. He wrapped his huge palms around her fingers and squeezed them gently.

"You idiot. I don't mean because of this injury. I mean because I'll miss you. Really miss you…" He paused and looked deep into her eyes.

"You'll miss me?" Carrie squawked in shocked delight. "I'll miss you too Dan." She lifted her face to look up at him.

He suddenly dropped her hands and slowly raised his to her face, touching her cheeks with his fingertips and leaning in close, his warm breath wafting over her.

And then his expression changed again. His fingers dropped from her face to her shoulder and he sat back again as he sighed deeply. He gave her shoulder one more quick rub as he spoke.

"Look, don't worry about it if you can't get out tomorrow, I'll come over to your place. I'll say I've already had the bug so your mum will have to let me in to visit my sick friend. We can do some exercises to get it moving then. Come on, I'm sending you home now so you can start pretending to be ill." He stood up quickly and pulled her up gently from the sofa.

Carrie stood looking up at him, but he avoided her gaze and turned abruptly towards the front door. She followed him, confusion curling through her stomach. She had been sure he had been about to kiss her a moment ago, and she wondered what had put him off. She tried to shrug, but stopped as she gasped in pain again. He turned quickly as he heard the stifled sound, but she smiled valiantly and walked past him as he opened the front door for her.

"You going to walk me up the road?" She asked as he came to a halt by the front gate. "Just in case I feel faint again." She added, the corner of her lip lifting as she spoke.

He grinned down at her.

"Do you feel faint then?" He took hold of her

hand and gave it a squeeze.

Carrie looked down as he intertwined his fingers with hers and she squeezed his hand back.

"Not really." She smiled. "But you never know with an injury like this, it might come over me all of a sudden. I wouldn't like to take any chances."

Daniel laughed and let go of her hand.

"I suppose so. Come on then." He walked out of the gate in front of her and they fell into step.

They only took a few minutes to cover the distance and they didn't speak again until they were almost at her gate. Just before they reached her house, he turned towards her and lifted his hand to her shoulder. He rubbed it gently and then picked up her hand. He turned it over in his and lifted her arm slightly, watching her face carefully for any signs of discomfort.

"Okay?" He asked, his eyes searching hers.

She nodded as she stared up at him, unable to speak again as she thought about him leaving. She gulped back the constriction in her throat.

"I'll give you a call later if everything is going to plan. What's your number?" She asked him quickly.

He fumbled in his pocket and brought out his mobile. He read out the number and then chuckled.

"Not many people have this. It's mostly only the team. You are highly honoured."

Carrie raised her eyebrows and laughed as she

tapped his number into her phone, but then her face fell again as an impatient hoot caused her to turn quickly.

They both stepped aside as Carrie's father pulled his car into the driveway and she deliberately ignored his furious expression as he glared angrily at Daniel.

Chapter Three
The Same Evening

"I don't believe her Helen. She's not sick. She's never sick. She didn't look sick earlier. I saw her holding hands with that great gorilla of a kid who lives up the road. The one that makes all that racket every night. She looked fine when she was making eyes at him. Goofy even… I thought he was gay for God's sake! I've never seen him with another girl. He's always hanging out with those other apes from the rugby team. She's puked up twice now. Christ! You don't think she's pregnant do you?"

Carrie fumed as she lay in bed listening to her father whispering loudly to her mother, just outside her bedroom door.

Her mother gave a startled gasp.

"Jim! How can you even think that? You should wash your mouth out with soap. That's our daughter's reputation you're maligning." Her mother sounded furious, and Carrie gave a grim smile before she settled her face into a martyred expression as she heard a gentle knock. Both her parents walked in through her door.

"Hey, sweetheart, how are you feeling now?" Her mother walked over to her bedside and laid a cool hand across her brow.

Carrie coughed dramatically, unsure of how convincing it sounded. She had never won a part in any of the school drama production.

"Awful. I was sick again ten minutes ago. I just want to go to sleep." Carrie kept her voice faint.

Helen glanced up at her husband before she concentrated on her daughter again.

"What have you eaten at school today, or did you have anything later at Daniel's house? Dad seems to think you were with him this afternoon." She sat down on the edge of the bed and Carrie thought hard about how to fend off the coming inquisition.

She gave her father a withering glare.

"I was only at Dan's because I felt a bit odd after the exam. You know, sort of light headed. He gave me a glass of water after we walked home, and then he came to the door with me just in case I felt faint, that's all. I thought it was just the stress of the exams but now I think it must be a bug. Daniel said he had it last week. He was ill for a couple of days. It wouldn't be so bad if it didn't make my head ache so much." Carrie fluttered her eyelids dramatically as she laid it on thick.

Jim pursed his lips, still looking unconvinced.

"Hmm, and you spend a lot of time with this Dan do you?" He frowned down at her.

Carrie shrugged and winced as she had a sudden reminder from her shoulder of why she was lying in bed faking being ill.

57

"Not that much. We walk to school together and sometimes home together too. We always have, right from primary school."

Her mother glanced up at her father.

"See Jim. I told you that you were making a mistake. There's nothing in it at all. Daniel was just bringing her home because she felt poorly. Isn't that nice of him?"

Jim was still frowning.

"Yes, well so long as it is just a bug. I don't want you mucking about with that great oaf Carrie. He looks dangerous to me. He obviously has enough hormones in him for the whole street."

Carrie struggled to sit up and defend Daniel.

"Dad, don't be ridiculous. He's my friend and I really like him. It's not his fault he's grown so big. His father is really tall too. You would hate it if someone didn't like you just because you're bald like grandpa. It's a hereditary thing not a failing."

Jim took a shocked breath and rubbed his hand self-consciously over his shining head.

"Now wait just a minute young lady! There's no reason to be so rude. I'm only saying that someone that huge is going to have trouble along-side him somewhere. I don't want you getting too involved. He's so massive his hormones must be running riot. He's got to have that much testosterone raging round him. He's going to have to give it an outlet sometime and for someone his age, that means either fighting or having sex. I don't want either of them to be with you, okay."

Carrie was outraged. She ignored the pain in her shoulder as she shot forwards.

"I don't think Daniel has ever had a fight in his life and I am certainly not having sex with him! I'm not having sex with anyone! Yet!" She added furiously. "Not that it's any of your business if I do. I am sixteen you know and it's quite legal, but just so you know, he's never even mentioned the subject to me. We've walked to and from school together almost every day since I was six. There's nothing in it at all." Carrie crossed her fingers under the duvet, desperately hoping that there would be. "He plays rugby or some other sport all the time. He gets rid of all his testos…stuff there. He's a really nice guy dad, and so are his mates. You shouldn't let appearances sway your opinion so easily."

Her father took a step back from Carrie's onslaught and raised his hands in surrender.

"Okay, I believe you, I'm sorry I spoke. You had better rest if you are going to rehearsals tomorrow. Antonio is going to be as mad as hell that you are going to miss tonight, better not make him madder."

Carrie was about to protest about the being sick rule when her mum spoke up for her.

"She can't go to rehearsals tomorrow either Jim.

They have to have forty-eight hours clear before they go back to training, otherwise it'll go round the group like wildfire. It's the warm, sweaty atmosphere in the studio that does it. It won't matter too much anyway, Carrie has the routine down to a tee. I'll give Antonio a call in a moment. Why don't you go and relax Jim, I'll be down in a jiffy."

Jim left the room after kissing Carrie on the forehead but her mum stayed sitting on the bed.

She waited until she heard the television downstairs and then she spoke to Carrie again.

"Are you really sick Carrie? You look a little flushed, but not ill and you don't have a temperature. Come on honey, you can tell me if anything's bothering you. You're not getting cold feet about the dancing are you?" She was full of concern.

Carrie smiled weakly and laid her head back on the pillows. She suddenly felt awful for being so deceitful. She couldn't meet her mother's gaze. Instead she made a big drama out of plumping the already plumped pillow.

"Don't be silly mum. I could do the dance standing on my head. I just feel ill, that's all."

But her mother wouldn't leave it.

"And Daniel? Are you telling us the truth about him." She flapped her hands as Carrie jumped forwards in the bed again. "Look, don't get mad at me. He's eighteen, he wouldn't be normal if he didn't have thoughts about sex. I just want to know that if anything is going on, that you're being safe. There's nothing like a baby to cramp your style."

Carrie had to laugh.

"Oh mum, was I that bad?"

Her mother shrugged and smiled.

"No, but then your dad is quite a bit older than me. He already had a good job and was able to provide for us all. I was quite happy to stay at home with you. This is a bit different for you, what with everything that's going on in your life. It's probably not a good time to have a relationship."

Carrie lay back on the pillows again and thought about the situation miserably.

"I know mum. Dan and I do like each other, but it's not going to go anywhere. He was just being kind 'cos I felt so ill. And anyway, he's going to America in September. He found out yesterday. He won a Sports Academy scholarship in Atlanta. It's fantastic for him, but it's a three year placement. We aren't going to be seeing each other for a very long while." Carrie covered her mouth with her hand as she nearly cried out with the intense pain that suddenly caught at her chest.

Her mum whipped up the bucket from the floor and Carrie made some convincing gagging noises and spat in it. She pulled a tissue from the box on her bedside table and made a big show of wiping her mouth.

Helen took the tissue and grimaced.

"Ewh! I think you've gone past bile now. You're gagging on nothing. That's so bad for you. Your stomach will be raw." Her mother looked into the bottom of the empty bucket. "Maybe you need something to eat. What about some buttered toast?"

Carrie moaned in longing. She was starving but she knew she would have to suffer for a few more hours if she were going to pull off this deception convincingly.

"Maybe later mum, I couldn't stomach anything at the moment. I'm just thirsty. Being sick has made my throat sore. Is there any coke?"

"I think there's a bottle in the fridge. I'll go and get you some. I'll give Antonio a quick ring and then bring a glass back up." She walked towards the door and closed it quietly behind her.

Carrie lay down and slipped her mobile phone out from under her pillow. She sent a quick text to Daniel, telling him how the first part of her plan was going, and had a smiley face reply within seconds. Then she put the phone back under the pillow as she heard her mother coming back up the stairs.

She handed Carrie the glass of coke and waited while Carrie sipped at it. Then she took the glass from her hand and put it on the bedside table.

"I'll leave that here in case you want any later. I

spoke to Antonio and he says you're to stay in bed for the next two days. He's going to come over on Saturday evening to see how you're getting on, but he's not rehearsing over the weekend anyway. I said you'd probably be okay for Monday, but he said don't come in until you're strong enough. If you're still weak, the dancing will make you worse. Better to have a few days off now than in the middle of the tour."

Carrie smiled in relief against the pillow, then lifted her head and spoke weakly.

"Thanks mum. I'm sure I'll be fine in a couple of days. Dan said it took him a while to get over it."

Her mother looked at her suspiciously one more time.

"Yes, I'm sure it did. Well, whatever it is wrong with you, I daresay he's going help you get over it. Your dad just saw him hanging around the gate still. He went out and asked him what he wanted. Apparently he says that he's coming over tomorrow to see if you're any better. Your dad says Daniel looks a lot sicker than you." Helen caught the hint of a smile that curled the corners of Carrie's mouth. She smiled indulgently as she walked back to the door and closed it gently behind her.

Chapter Four
The Next Day

Jim stood at the bottom of the stairs, staring up at the closed door of Carrie's bedroom. He dropped his briefcase outside the under-stair cupboard and slipped out of his jacket, then he took a deep breath and walked through to the kitchen.

Helen looked up at him in surprise.

"Whatever are you doing home so early?" She smiled as she walked over to him and wrapped her arms around his waist, then gave him a brief kiss on the lips.

He didn't kiss her back.

"Is that great oaf still here?" He looked down at his wife, his expression hard.

Helen let go of him quickly and stood back.

"Is that why you've come home early? Just to check up on them?" She turned back to the cooker and lifted the lid of the saucepan. "And I thought you had made the effort to see me! I wish I hadn't rung you to tell you he was here. You're being far too suspicious." She poked a knife into the contents of the saucepan.

Jim stepped up behind her and gave her a belated kiss on the cheek.

"I don't see why I shouldn't be suspicious. I'll swear that kid's on steroids. It can't be normal to be that huge. His parents aren't that tall, well his mother isn't at any rate...It'll be a disaster if she gets pregnant by him when she's only sixteen. Her life will be over. Nobody likes a teenage mum. Makes them cheap." His words were hard.

Helen put the knife down firmly on the worktop.

"Well, thanks for that Jim. Maybe you have forgotten but I was pregnant at sixteen. It's nice to know you think I'm cheap." She moved along the kitchen units, grabbed the knife again and began peeling the carrots vigorously.

Jim sighed wearily and moved up close behind his wife. He ignored the knife being wielded expertly along the carrots.

"I didn't mean you. I love you now and I loved you then. I knew you were the one for me...It's just all so different now-a-days. Everyone has to have a career and Carrie has been given the chance of a fabulous one. I just don't want it all ruined for her by that great lumbering kid. Do you even know what they're up to in there?"

Helen gave a resigned sigh. He obviously wasn't going to let this go.

"They were listening to some music when I took them a drink an hour ago. He was sitting on the floor by the end of her bed, fully dressed, including his trainers, and no-where near Carrie." Helen added the carrots to the saucepan. "I've asked him if he wants to stop for dinner, so you'd better put on a pleasanter

65

manner before they come down or he's going to think you're a right grumpy old git."

Jim groaned and rolled his eyes.

"What the hell were you doing encouraging him?" He sighed, his shoulder drooping in resignation. "I'm going to get changed. Why don't we eat outside? The weather's nice enough and he won't be quite so overpowering out in the garden."

Helen nodded and turned back to the cooking.

Jim trudged to the stairs and then, making sure that the kitchen door was shut, he crept quickly up them and stood listening outside Carrie's door. He heard voices inside. Daniel's was low and rumbling.

"Perfect Carrie. Spread them wide, wider, go on, I know you can do it. Now lift this one higher, yes, see I can push you further, and another deep breath. That's right, I want you to really feel it. Relax your whole body now." There was a short pause, then. "Perfect, you're loosening up nicely. I told you it wouldn't hurt if we went slowly."

Jim's eyes grew wide and he bent his head closer to the door, listening hard. He heard Carrie's higher pitched voice. She sounded breathy, almost lazy.

"That feels so good Daniel, it's really hard, but when you push gently I can get it nearly all the way up, much higher than I thought would be possible. I've never done anything like this before. The deeper I breathe, the more I can take. You must have had a lot of experience with this sort of thing."

Daniel's deep rumbling laugh came back as the floorboards creaked in a gentle rhythm.

"Only once or twice before Carrie, and you are the first one to take so much. It's just a matter of taking things slow and easy. I don't want to hurt you. You have to be really relaxed. It's no good at all if you're too tense, but you've managed to do it for well over half an hour. Not everyone can take it this hard the first time, but you are so flexible you make it look easy. Are you feeling good? I don't want this to hurt you. Tell me if it's too much." There was a short pause and then Carrie answered.

"No, it's fine." Then a great sigh. "Oh wow! I can feel that deep inside."

Daniel grunted as the floorboards creaked.

"Not too fast Carrie. There's plenty of time. We don't have to rush this. I can come again tomorrow if you want me to. We'll keep it gentle so you have time to get used to the different positions and I promise that it'll feel even better the second time. There's no way you can take in all of this the first time, so we'll work slowly and as soon as you're ready we can really get into a rhythm. We'll see if we can work it all the way up tomorrow, maybe even try it from the other way round. Bending over forwards and arching your back sometimes makes it easier."

Carrie moaned a little and then sighed deeply.

"Yeah, I think that would be a great idea. I'm not averse to experimenting. I mean, I'm obviously pleased I've done so well today, but you must be disappointed that it's still so stiff. I bet you would have preferred it if I had been able to go all the way with it. You know, released it completely."

Daniel's voice rumbled through the door.

"Try not to worry Carrie, I'm a very patient guy. There's a lot to take in and I'm satisfied with what we have done today. I wouldn't expect anyone to manage it all the first time. If I'm really gentle with you, we'll probably be able to go the whole way tomorrow. I don't want to hurt you by going too far too fast."

Jim stood up straight. His cheeks were purple with rage. He had heard enough. He didn't care how big the animal was, he couldn't let him ruin his daughter.

He grasped the door handle and shoved hard, putting all his weight behind his shoulder as he rammed the wooden panel at the same time, just in case the door was locked.

It wasn't. He burst into the room and almost tripped over Carrie who was sitting cross legged on the floor with her back towards the door. He swerved to avoid a collision and fell headlong onto the bed, his momentum crashing him into the opposite wall. He slid off the bed sideways, momentarily stunned, and landed in Daniel's lap. He struggled to free himself from a tangle of huge, long legs and massive feet as Daniel took hold of his shoulders and sat him up straight.

"You okay there, Mr. Denton? Do you want to join in?" Daniel looked more than surprised.

Jim was still purple.

"Why you filthy!…" Jim shouted and wrenched himself out of Daniel's grasp, his whole body shaking with almost uncontrollable anger.

Then he suddenly shut his mouth as he saw that Daniel was at least six feet from Carrie. They were both fully dressed including their trainers, exactly as Helen had described. Carrie was glaring furiously at him, her arms stretched above her head. He blustered as Daniel stood up gracefully and stuck his hand out to pull Jim from the floor. Jim frowned for a moment, then took it begrudgingly, his eyes opening wide again as he took in Daniel's bulging biceps.

"What are you both doing? What's going on in here?" His tone was still accusing.

Daniel smiled easily at him, but then glanced at Carrie quickly as she moved her arms to put them down. He spoke quickly.

"No! Don't stop yet," He warned as he made gentling motions with his huge hands. "Extend the stretch first, that's right…make sure your breath comes out fully. And slowly bring them back down. Okay, you can relax now." He gave Carrie instructions before turning to her father again. "Sorry about that Mr. Denton. I didn't want Carrie to cut the stretch short. There are a lot of instructions to follow and it can be easy to forget the vital one."

Jim raised his eyebrows quizzically as he brushed carpet fluff from his trousers and straightened his shirt.

"Instructions for what exactly?"

Daniel smiled widely, obviously keen to share his favourite subject.

"I'm showing Carrie my new form of workout. I've designed it especially for sportsmen and women who are sick or injured, but need to keep their fitness up. I thought it would be a good idea for her while she's poorly. You know, so she doesn't feel sluggish when she goes back to the dancing. Three or four days without exercise can make a huge difference to someone as fit as Carrie. It's based on yoga, but there's a lot more to it than that. Deep breathing skills are really important so you get a really good work out without wearing yourself out. I'm hoping to launch it in America when I go to college in September. It's going to be a major part of my thesis." His enthusiasm was more than genuine.

Jim smiled lamely and then turned bright red as he saw his wife shaking her head at him from the landing.

Carrie pulled her arms up over her head again, breathed in deeply and then relaxed back down. She was still glaring at her father as she rolled her shoulders gently.

"And it was working too, until you burst in and nearly bashed me on the back of my head. Whatever were you thinking of dad? You only had to knock if you wanted to join us." She said sarcastically.

Jim sidled out of the doorway.

"No, no, I just tripped at the top of the stairs. I grabbed the door handle so I didn't fall over…I'll leave you to it." He stuck his thumbs up at Daniel. "Sounds good Daniel, it'll be an excellent thesis I'm sure. Keep it up." He walked quickly across the landing to his bedroom. Helen followed him closely. She closed the door behind her and turned on her husband.

"How embarrassing Jim! They weren't doing anything wrong. You're lucky Carrie didn't show you right up. Maybe she thought you'd done enough by yourself, you great idiot. If you ever do anything like that again, I shall make you apologize properly and then you'll really know what embarrassing is."

Carrie was still sitting cross legged on the floor. She rubbed her shoulder hard as she looked at the carpet, her cheeks as bright red as her fathers.

"I am so sorry Dan. He must have been listening at the door and thought we were up to something. What an idiot."

Daniel came over to her and brushed her hand away from her shoulder.

"Parent's eh? It's okay. I guess I'd be worried if I was the father of a beautiful young girl, who had got a massive great lump of a bloke in her bedroom. It's good that he cares about you." He knelt down behind her and laid his huge hands on her shoulder. He began massaging firmly.

"Maybe" She answered as she relaxed completely and felt her body moving in rhythm with his massage. "But he's still an idiot.

Carrie's T-shirt sleeve started riding up with the movement and Daniel's hot hands touched her bare skin. She hung her head, pretending to stretch her neck as his heat worked through her body. It was almost impossible to keep calm. All she wanted to do was to reach round, throw her arms around his neck and kiss him passionately.

"Hmm…Your hands are so warm Dan, it's like having a heat treatment on my shoulder. I'm surprised how much I can do already." She tried to keep her voice neutral as she rolled her arm in its socket.

Daniel moved his hands to the back of her neck. Carrie could feel his breath in her hair and she let out a small groan of pleasure.

He dropped his hands and moved away from her.

"We've done enough for today. I don't want you

to overdo it. It's obviously painful still." Daniel stood up quickly and moved towards the door. "We can do a little more with it tomorrow if you don't go too stiff overnight. Make sure you take a hot bath later and keep it moving tonight, but do it gently, okay. Don't do anything that pulls it tight."

Carrie stood up too, wishing that she had managed to take control of her voice box as easily as she could control her body.

"Sure, anything you say, come on, I bet dinner is ready by now. I'll come down too and have just a small plate full, just to keep up the appearance of being ill still."

Daniel looked a little concerned.

"Do you think I should stay? Your dad didn't look very happy to see me here, even after he knew everything was okay. I don't want to upset him or anything."

Carrie laughed and caught hold of Daniel's arm. She pulled him to her side.

"There's no way you are letting my dad off the hook tonight. He's going to have to pay big time for that intrusion and the filthy thoughts he had about what we were doing. I can't believe he had the nerve to burst in like that. At least it will teach him not to listen at doors. No, you're staying whether you like it or not, just to make him feel really uncomfortable if nothing else."

Daniel laughed with her.

"Okay, but don't say anything over the dinner table about it. I'm embarrassed too you know."

Carrie looked up at him and arched her eyebrows.

"You don't have anything to be embarrassed about."

Daniel looked a little sheepish.

"Of course I do. Any normal eighteen year old would have been trying it on with you. He probably thinks I'm a right weirdo now."

"Daniel!" Carrie exclaimed and blushed furiously again. "Now I'm embarrassed too. I think we'd better shut up on the subject." She started down the stairs with Daniel just a step behind her, their conversation whirling around in her head.

She suddenly felt her heart sinking as she reached the bottom step. Daniel really hadn't tried anything on with her at all. *Was he telling her that he wasn't normal?*

She thought through their day together. He shown her, on the internet, where his placement would be in America and they had listened to their favourite bands while talking about their futures. They had been alone together in her bedroom for nearly eight hours and he hadn't done a thing to make her think he liked her any more than as a friend.

They had had a perfectly normal conversation

and he had helped her with her exercises, once that morning and again just before her father had interrupted them. He had barely even massaged her shoulder. Even he had admitted himself that it wasn't normal behaviour for an eighteen year old.

The realization of what he was saying suddenly swept over her. It was so obvious now.

Daniel really was gay! Her father had been right.

The little things he'd said and done before leapt into her brain. It was his way of telling her he wasn't interested in her, or other women for that matter. All that stuff he had said about missing her the day before and thinking that he was going to kiss her, was all just him being a sensitive gay bloke.

Carrie nearly cried out in frustration. How could the biggest, most handsome guy in the whole world, the only one she had ever loved, would ever love, be gay?

It just wasn't fair.

She set her expression as she reached the hallway. Well, even if he was gay, she wasn't going to not be with him. Not now they were getting on so well. Okay, so it wasn't going to go anywhere, but she could still see him.

And then her heart sank again. Even though the summer holidays were coming up, she was going to be so busy she would hardly have a moment at home and then he would be going to America for at least three years. She felt her face crumple and her throat constrict. There was a burning knot in her stomach that she couldn't shift. She stopped dead in the hall and Daniel bumped into the back of her, nearly knocking her flying.

"You okay?" He asked over her shoulder, suddenly concerned.

"No" She whispered as she shook her head. "I think I really do feel ill after all. I don't think I can eat any dinner." Her voice was shaking.

Daniel came round in front of her and bent to look in her eyes.

"Perhaps we overdid it with the exercises. It's not an exact science. You're not in any pain are you?" He was so close that she could feel his breath on her face.

She couldn't trust her voice. It felt as though her throat was full of splinters. She shook her head.

And then a tear spilt down her cheek. She felt so desolate that for a moment she didn't try to stop it, and after the first tear had escaped from the corner of her eye, a positive deluge seemed to follow. She wiped her face with the back of her hand and tried to stop them as she saw Daniel standing there staring at her, looking appalled.

He suddenly whipped out a tissue from his pocket and handed it to her. She sniffed into it and wiped some more tears.

"Carrie, what's the matter?" He asked, his voice so gentle she almost cried some more.

She shrugged awkwardly and stammered for a few seconds as she gulped back the tears.

"I…I don't know Dan. I just feel sort of odd, almost lonely. I keep on thinking about this tour. Maybe I'm just homesick already." She covered herself as quickly as she could and then Daniel did the worst thing possible.

He stepped even closer to her, lifted his arms to her shoulders and pulled her into his chest. She could feel his heart thumping and hear his breath filling his lungs. His huge arms were so warm around her, his hands pressing into the small of her back. She sank against him, moulding her body to his, thinking that if this was all he could ever give her, she was going to take as much of it as she could. He rested his chin on top of her head and they just stood there for a while, not speaking, not doing anything at all and then Daniel lifted his head again. He kept hold of her as he spoke softly.

"I'm homesick already too. I'm going to miss everyone so much. At least you get to come back here after the summer. I'm going to be somewhere where I won't know a soul except Paul, for at least three years, and if I don't like it there or don't do well, then I'm going to have to work like crazy to get back home because I can only afford a one way flight."

Carrie looked up at him, blinking her eyes dry.

"Oh Dan. Don't sound so miserable please. You know it's what you want to do. It's a once in a lifetime chance, a fantastic opportunity, you have to take it. You would be completely mad not to. And then there's Paul. How will he feel if you suddenly back out of it? You'll make friends easily enough. Everyone loves you here, it'll be no different there."

Daniel let go of her suddenly and spoke bitterly.

"I don't want everyone to love me, Carrie. I only want…" He paused and took a deep breath. "It's okay, I'm not backing out of it. I just wish I had more time to think, to do the right thing…" He tailed off, stepped back and looked down at her for a long moment, his ocean blue eyes wandering over her face, her hair, her body. Then he looked up again as he heard the sound of pots clattering coming from the kitchen. "Come on, I'm hungry and as you haven't eaten since yesterday, you must be starving too. We mustn't keep your parents waiting. I don't want them thinking any worse of me." He caught hold of Carrie's hand and gave it a quick squeeze before he let it go again and turned towards the kitchen.

Chapter Five
September 1st 2007

"Can't we make it home tonight Antonio? Do we have to stay another night? I really need to get back as soon as possible. Can't Lisa or Derek drive?" Carrie knew she was clutching at straws, but she was willing to try anything to spend an extra day with Daniel.

Antonio glared at her.

"No they can't. It's a hire bus and they do not have insurance, apart from the fact they are just as tired as I am. For goodness sake Carrie, we've been on the road all day today. I had no idea Scotland was so huge. I'm absolutely shattered. One more night in a hotel won't kill you, which is something I may do if I don't get some sleep soon. This tour has been harder work than I imagined. I hadn't reckoned on all the extra publicity stuff. I assumed that it was just the concerts that we'd be doing. God! How wrong can you be! Serves me right for not checking the small print." His voice was strained.

They had stopped in a Birmingham hotel and Carrie felt even more frustrated as she knew that they could be in London in less than three hours.

She sent Daniel a text and gave him the bad news. She expected him to text back, but she was surprised when a few seconds later her mobile rang displaying an unknown number. Lisa, lead dancer with the group, was looking over her shoulder. She nudged Carrie hard with her elbow and nodded her head vigorously.

Carrie pressed the receive button. It was Daniel.

"Hey, Carrie, I'm on Paul's mobile. I've been an idiot and left mine at home. We guessed Antonio would be knackered." There was a lot of background traffic noise and then he spoke again. "Paul called Lisa a while back and we set out more or less straight away. Paul said he couldn't wait another day to see her. We'll be with you in less than an hour. "

Carrie nearly cried with happiness.

"Well thank goodness for that. I thought I was only going to get one day to see you." She spoke softly, not really wanting the others to hear. Paul and Daniel had come to two of the concerts, to watch them dance, during the summer and Paul and Lisa had been getting on very well together.

"I can't wait to see you Carrie." Daniel said suddenly.

"Me either." She replied. Although Daniel had said nothing to get her hopes up during the summer months, she felt very close to him. Even though she suspected he was gay, she never spoke about it with him and she never spoke about their relationship either. She didn't want to spoil what she had. "See you in an hour."

Her phone clicked off and she sat back, smiling

80

widely, in the lounge chair.

Antonio looked up at her.

"Happy now lover boy's on his way?" He smiled at her indulgently. At sixteen she was the youngest in the group by a couple of years, but they had all become pretty close over the summer.

She nodded and then shook her head quickly.

"Of course I'm happy, but he's not my lover, so don't go mentioning that will you. He won't like it."

Antonio gave a great guffaw.

"Well, you could have fooled me. He looked like a dog in heat when he last came to see you. I thought it was in the bag."

Carrie stuck her nose up in the air, slightly disgusted with his turn of phrase.

"Well, you thought wrong then Antonio. You must have got him mixed up with Paul. He's obviously fallen for Lisa big time." She ignored her friend's mad giggling at her side. "Daniel's not like that. We're just really good friends. In fact I would say he is my best friend."

Antonio shook his head as the corner of his mouth twitched upwards.

"Okay, if that's how you want to play it, that's fine by me. I'm just glad he's got you off my back that's all. Now come on, we can sort out the rooms." The rest of the group crowded round as he paired them off. "You and Lisa can go in together, but I don't want

81

those two blokes of yours trying to bunk in with you. They'll either have to book themselves another room or go home." Antonio looked straight at Lisa with a meaningful stare.

She stuck her tongue out at him and then spoke up quickly.

"They're leaving late on. Paul wants to spend as much time as possible with his little sister. She's only twelve and she's really cut up about him going off to America, so he's trying to fit everything in. They're going to leave around midnight."

Antonio nodded and then yawned so widely Carrie thought he might dislocate his jaw.

"Well, you lot may want to stay up until then, but I can tell you that I'm going to have something to eat and then hit the sack. Don't forget to bring me bills if you want your dinner refunded out of expenses and please stick within our budget. Just remember that it doesn't cover any alcohol." He rolled his eyes at a grinning Callum and Toby, then started giving out the room cards. The others all went to find their rooms but Carrie and Lisa ordered some drinks and sat in the lounge. They had struck up a firm friendship over the last six weeks. Carrie had even confided to her new friend that she was in love with Daniel, even though she knew it was hopeless.

"He's never even tried to kiss me. A while back, when I hurt my arm, I thought he was going to, but I must have been mistaken." Carrie had also confessed to Lisa about her shoulder injury. "We spent five days in my bedroom at the beginning of the summer doing this exercise regime he's thought up, and he never once did anything to make me think he fancied me. It's hopeless really, but if he wants to be my friend, then that's okay with me. I'd rather see him just sometimes than not at all."

Carrie looked out into the car park to see if she could see Paul's car arriving.

Lisa caught her friend's hand.

"Are you sure he's gay though? He doesn't seem like it to me. I swear that Paul would have known and said something to me if he suspected anything like that. If you hadn't told me, I'd never have believed it for a moment."

Carrie shrugged.

"He just isn't out of the closet yet. Maybe he thinks it'll damage his chances in America. But it's not just that. I've never seen him go out with any girl, or if he has he's kept it very quiet. I mean, I've seen him nearly every day since I was six. You'd think I'd notice if he had a girlfriend hanging on his arm." She felt the familiar knot of misery in her stomach and then suddenly Lisa was bouncing up out of her chair.

"They're here! Look, they're parking over there. God, he must have been driving like the devil to get here that fast. I bet the idiot has a speeding ticket coming in the post." She giggled madly.

Carrie grinned as she stood up.

"Just as well he's going to America then. They might not catch up with him there…Aren't you going to miss Paul terribly when he's gone?" Carrie hadn't dared to ask before, but now seeing her friend's delighted expression as she could see Paul climbing from the car, Carrie felt able to wonder out loud.

Lisa waved to Paul through the window. His face lit up as he saw her and he and Daniel began to jog towards the hotel entrance. They looked like two giants as their huge feet ate up the gravel and one or two other guests quickly stepped out of their way. Knowing how soft the two of them were, Carrie couldn't help smiling as one lady appeared to shudder as they ran past her.

Lisa was still chattering excitedly.

"He says he's going to send for me as soon as he's settled. He's going to get a job so that we can live together. I can't wait."

Carrie gasped, shocked to the core.

"But what about the dancing? Our contract! You're only nineteen. You can't mean you're going to give it all up yet. And what about the money? What will you do out there?"

Lisa was looking dewy eyed at Paul as he strode through the foyer and into the lounge.

"I've been dancing for as long as I can remember. I love it still, but this touring is awful. I've been with a couple of other bands and it's always the same. Damned hard work and the money is rubbish. We all only do it because we love it so much. I tell you Carrie, if you want to get rich, then don't ever be a dancer, go be a lawyer. Anyway, that scarcely matters, as much as I love dancing I'd give it up in an instant if it meant being with him for the rest of my life…but as it happens, I don't think it'll come to that. I'm sure I can get a job out there, what with this tour on my C.V. At the very least I'll be able to teach in a dance school."

Lisa ran towards Paul and melted into his outstretched arms as he reached for her. The next second she was enveloped in his huge chest, held tightly to his body while he kissed her passionately.

Daniel rolled his eyes at Carrie and she smiled back at him as he came over and gave her a quick peck on the cheek. She closed her eyes for just a second and breathed in his delicious scent. He caught hold of her hand as he moved towards the bar.

"All right Carrie? I told you we wouldn't be long. What are you two drinking?" His voice was as deep and as soft as normal and Carrie fought back the urge to launch herself at him and kiss him as enthusiastically as Lisa was kissing Paul.

"Just mineral water thanks, and the same for Lisa. She looks like she's going to be thirsty. Paul must have been desperate to see her if he's driven all this way, just to go back again tonight." She nodded over her shoulder at the still kissing pair. Paul looked as though he was eating Lisa and Carrie had to put her hand over her mouth to stop herself laughing out loud.

Daniel looked down at her. He didn't answer her until he had ordered two coffees and two mineral waters.

"Yeah, he's got it bad and he just can't keep it under control. He's going to be sorry if he can't afford to bring her out to the States or if she decides she doesn't want to come."

He picked up the tray of drinks and walked towards a table while Carrie trailed behind him.

"Not much chance of that. She's desperate to get out there with him. She'd go right now if he gave her the chance. She even said she'd give up dancing." Carrie sat facing away from the still kissing couple.

Daniel looked across at her, his deep blue eyes searching her grey ones. Then they flicked up and glanced over her shoulder to the amorous pair once more.

"Would you give up your dancing to go? If it was someone you really loved who asked you, I mean?" He asked suddenly, his eyes burning into hers.

Carrie gulped at their intensity and her heart soared. She didn't need to think.

"Yes of course, if the right person asked me, I'd do anything for them." She stared back at Daniel, willing him to ask her, but he just glanced over at Paul and Lisa again and then picked up his coffee cup and blew on the hot liquid before speaking.

"You're only sixteen Carrie. You'd be mad to go and ruin your chances of a decent career if you don't take your 'A' levels. You would be much better off working hard to get your qualifications. You should wait until whoever it was came back and had enough money to support both of you, just in case anything goes wrong. I mean, look at my mum and dad. They hate each other's guts, but they can't afford to do a thing about it. I think you need to have a good education and plenty of money so you both have the best chances in life before you do anything permanent...Hey Paul, your coffee is going cold!" He yelled towards his friend, then sat back in his chair and scowled furiously as Paul came up for air at last and dragged Lisa over to the table.

"Sorry about that, just making up for lost time." Paul sat down and pulled Lisa onto his lap. She squealed delightedly, but then shifted herself to sit on the seat beside him as two elderly ladies at the next table gasped in horror, scandalized by their outrageous behaviour.

"Paul, you idiot, we're in a hotel, not a holiday camp. Show a little decorum please." But she was still giggling as she said it. She picked up her mineral water and put a straw in the glass. "Thanks Daniel. Not long before you're off now. You all packed and ready to go?" She took a long suck of the water through the straw, fluttering her eyelashes at Paul as she did so. Paul watched her lips avidly, then flung himself back in his seat and groaned loudly.

Daniel shot him another glare, then turned to Lisa.

"Just about. I didn't realize how little twenty kilo's is. I've cut everything to the bare minimum, but I'm still over the baggage limit. It's not fair, we're both going to have to pay a supplement. I think allowances should be made for people as big as Paul and me, all our clothes are so much bigger and weigh more than average. I'm not taking any jumpers or heavy trousers, only two pairs of trainers and I shall be wearing one of them. I'm hoping to get a job fairly soon so I can buy some more clothes. After all, if we're going to be there nearly three years, I'm going to need more than a suitcase full."

Paul sipped his coffee, pulled a face at the bitter taste and then heaped in three spoons of sugar. He stirred vigorously.

"We won't need to worry Dan. I'm sure we're both going to get picked for the Atlanta Raiders and we're going to make our fortunes." He squeezed Lisa to his side. "We've already arranged tryouts, but Dan likes to take the worst possible view of any situation."

Daniel grunted.

"Yeah, and you're ever the optimist. It'll be a miracle if we get picked. They must have hundreds of guys just like us trying out every year. I don't think we're going to stand out that much." He sipped his own coffee as he looked over to Carrie. "Glad the tour's over?"

Carrie nodded.

"It's been such hard work. I knew it was going to be tough going, but when the band said they are doing seven gigs, that's pretty much it apart from a couple of publicity shoots. Yeah they might sit about and strum a guitar on the odd occasion, but we dancers have to train every single day for hours. It's absolutely shattering." She slumped back in her seat.

Daniel leaned forwards and rested his elbows on his knees.

"Don't forget to use those exercises you learned to help you relax. They're not just for injuries, though I have to confess, you made an excellent recovery from the shoulder thing. Have you spoken to that old bat that did it to you?"

Carrie shook her head as she took a sip of the water.

"No. I wouldn't call her and she certainly wouldn't speak to me if I did. It's better now, so there's no harm done. I don't know if I'll be seeing her again anyway. I hear she's not coming back to the college. Someone said she's having a go at journalism."

Daniel finished his coffee.

"Good, so long as she's not anywhere near you. She's dangerous." He finished firmly.

Paul was eyeing Lisa again. She put her hand up to her hair and smoothed it where Paul had ruffled her in his earlier enthusiastic embrace.

Lisa sat up straight and moved away from Paul slightly as she saw Antonio trudge wearily out of the restaurant. He looked exhausted as he nodded in their direction and then made his way towards the lift. Lisa snuggled against Paul again.

"Are we eating together, because if we are going to the restaurant, I need to change my clothes. I only wore this for travelling." She looked down at her sloppy grey t-shirt and purple tracksuit bottoms.

Paul grinned immediately and waggled his eyebrows at her.

"Want any help with that?"

Carrie sighed as Lisa fell about in fits of laughter. She glanced down at her own comfortable black sweatpants. They were more fitted than Lisa's purple sloppies and her white t-shirt still looked pristine. She looked across to Daniel. He looked fabulous wearing pale denim jeans with a snugly fitting black t-shirt. She shrugged, not wanting to make a big thing of it.

"I'm not worried what I look like. I'm going in

as I am. You hungry Dan?"

Daniel laughed and stood up. He pulled himself up straight and puffed out his huge chest.

"What do you think? I can always eat. Are we waiting for you two?" He glanced down at Paul, who couldn't seem to take his eyes off Lisa.

Paul waved him away without looking up.

"No, you two go ahead. If Lisa wants to go and get changed then that's fine by me. Gives me time to phone my baby sister. She's left me about twenty messages already and if I don't get back to her soon, I'll never hear the last of it. She'll torture me even if I am thousands of miles away." He stood up. "We'll catch up with you two later maybe."

Lisa gave them a wave as she headed for the lift. Paul kept his eyes fixed on her as he keyed in numbers on his phone. Lisa looked back at him over her shoulder, fluttering her eyelashes and he stopped pressing the buttons. He put the phone back in his pocket and strode after Lisa as she waited by the lift door.

Daniel shook his head in resignation and steered Carrie towards the restaurant.

"We'll let them have a romantic evening together shall we?" He smiled at Carrie. "We can have something to eat and then go out onto the terrace. It's still warm enough to sit outside I think, if you want to that is?" His eyes questioned her.

Carrie looked down at the floor, suddenly embarrassed. It felt as though he was asking her out on a date.

"That would be lovely Dan. We can have coffee out there after we've eaten."

They walked through to the restaurant and were soon laughing as Daniel quickly demolished half a dozen grilled king prawns then a huge plate of deliciously creamy pasta, plus the uneaten half of Carrie's too. Afterwards he devoured apple pie and custard followed by a whole plate of cheese and biscuits.

The waiter, clearly impressed with Daniel's ability to appreciate good food, showed them to seats on the terrace and left an extra-large coffee pot and a whole box of after dinner chocolates on the table.

Carrie sat back in her chair and stared out over the lake beside them. The darkening sky and the evening lights were reflected in its mirror surface. It was so romantic that she nearly cried out in frustration as Daniel began peeling the foil from a chocolate. He passed it to her then began pouring coffee for the two of them. She nibbled the chocolate for a moment, but Daniel took it from her fingers and dipped it in the coffee.

He smiled at her quizzical look.

"I think they dip their chocolate in Europe. It's supposed to bring out the flavour more when it's warm." He passed the slightly melted chocolate back to her.

She let the chocolate dissolve slowly in her mouth then took a gulp of the hot coffee and settled back in the chair again. Daniel picked up another chocolate, his long fingers surprisingly delicate as he unwrapped the dark circle. He offered it to her, but she shook her head. The lump in her throat threatened to cut off her airways and she found herself shivering as she tried to keep her emotions at bay.

"You cold?" Daniel asked as he put the chocolate in his own mouth.

"A bit." She managed to stammer. And then Daniel stood up and pulled her from the chair and onto his lap. He wrapped his long arms right around her body and hugged her into his chest.

"Better?" He asked after a few moments, resting his chin on the top of her head. She could smell the chocolate on his breath, dark and delicious.

She nodded into his warm body.

"Much. You're always so warm." She could feel him smile above her.

He wrapped his shoulders around her as she snuggled in.

"Do you want to go inside? I don't mind." His voice was so close to her ear that she shivered violently again. He began to stand up, lifting her with him.

"No, no." She sounded almost panicked. "It's too

lovely out here. I'll be fine in a mo. I think I'm just really tired."

She felt Daniel relax back and his arms moved comfortably around her, holding her gently as he rubbed his hands up and down her bare skin.

"Yes, you must all be after a tour like that."

Carrie leaned her head against his hard shoulder and she felt him take a deep breath. His heart was thumping hard inside his chest. It was a quick, steady beat, probably a little quicker than it should have been. Maybe it needed to pump that fast to move the blood around his gigantic frame.

A cool breeze wafted up from the lake. She closed her eyes and snuggled against him again, listening to his heartbeat and his gentle breathing, smelling the subtly fragranced skin at his neck and rubbing her forehead on the day old stubble on his chin.

"You haven't shaved." She mumbled as she stifled a yawn.

His soft laughter rumbled through his chest.

"Couldn't be asked this afternoon. When Paul decided we were coming to meet you, we didn't bother stopping to worry about a bit of facial hair. You don't mind do you?" He rubbed his chin lightly against her cheek.

She was barely able to speak as her whole body began to shiver involuntarily. The words came out as a hoarse whisper.

"No, of course not. I'm just glad you came. But I expect it to be gone by the time I see you tomorrow. I don't want you to go to America looking scruffy. It'll create a bad first impression." She yawned again wishing she hadn't brought up the subject of his imminent departure.

He suddenly held her even tighter.

"I'll shave in the morning." He spoke quietly and then looked up as the sound of familiar high pitched laughter and an equally familiar answering growl reached their ears from an open upstairs window. There was the swooshing sound of the window sliding closed and then the silent evening closed in around them.

Carrie didn't realize that she had fallen asleep until she was being wakened as she was laid in her bed. Daniel leaned down, undid her trainers and tugged them gently off her feet, then he pulled the cool covers over her and tucked them round her body. She dragged them into her chest as he stood up and moved back from the bed.

She turned over to face him.

"Oh, sorry. Did you carry me up?" She tried to sit up, but Daniel placed his hand on her shoulder and pushed her back down.

"Go back to sleep Carrie. It's really late and Paul

and I have to go. We can't stay any longer. I'll see you, okay?" His deep voice swept over her.

Carrie laid back, yawned lazily and snuggled into the pillow.

"Night Dan. See you in the morning." She closed her eyes as he replied in a whisper.

"Night Carrie. See you."

His voice was husky in her ear and she felt a warm breath near her cheek. There was one last waft of his delicious scent before the door clicked closed and he was gone from the room.

Chapter Six
Lunchtime September 2nd

Carrie leapt into her father's arms as he crowded around the tour bus with the rest of the clamouring parents.

"Hey dad, it's great to see you. Where's mum?" Carrie looked around, after she had kissed his cheek, hoping to see Daniel too, but the car-park was just full of excited families.

Jim put her back down after swinging her around.

"She's at home cooking you a welcome home dinner for tonight. We're having a bit of a celebration seeing as you've not been here all summer and you go back to college next week. Half the street is coming."

Carrie groaned.

"Oh no! How embarrassing. What are you doing that for? I just want a quiet night in." *With Daniel preferably,* she thought privately. He was leaving the next day and she wanted to spend as much time with him as possible.

Her father grinned.

"Don't be silly. The tour was a brilliant success. Everyone wants to see the most famous kid
in our street. They all want to say well done. Helen and I have missed you terribly. We want to celebrate now that you're home. Now, don't you going and being a

misog about it, your mother has been to a lot of trouble."

Carrie let out an even deeper groan.

"Okay, but I'm absolutely shattered, you'll have to forgive me if I don't stay up too late." She wondered how soon she was going to be able to sneak off and see Daniel in private.

Jim picked up her duffel bag and headed for the car.

"Yes well, you're going to have to be in bed early for the next few nights. College begins in two days. You will have a lot of work to do for the next two years. It's really important that you keep up with your education, even if the dancing is giving you a bit of an income already. At least you won't be distracted by that great oaf, Daniel. I have to confess Carrie, I was glad to see the back of him. You don't need anyone like that interfering in your life."

Carrie had been trailing behind. She stopped dead for a moment and then rushed after him again.

"What do you mean dad? You have invited him tonight haven't you?"

Jim opened the boot of the car and put the case inside.

"Your mother did last week, but there was a last minute change of plans. He left for America with that other huge chum of his last night, so he's not going to be here to bother you anymore anyway. He came round to tell us as they were leaving just so your mother didn't prepare any food especially. Pretty decent of him really, considering how much he can eat. I think your mum halved the quantity of what she was cooking. No, we're going to have everything back to normal from now on." Jim smiled widely and opened the car door for her.

Carrie's feet were rooted to the spot.

"What do you mean, left last night? He's supposed to be seeing me today." Her chest felt as though a thick band of elastic was being wrapped around it, constricting her breathing to the point at which she thought she was going to pass out.

Her father was still smiling stupidly.

"No, he definitely went yesterday. I know because he came to say goodbye. He and that other huge bloke had all their bags in the car. Apparently they had managed to get an earlier flight out of Birmingham that cost less than half of flying from Heathrow. Daniel seemed to think what they saved would cover the cost of their first month's rent on campus. They had to check in at Birmingham at about two in the morning. Your mum offered to pack them a load of the food she had been preparing but they said they were going to have dinner in some hotel up there before they went on the airport. That other bloke said his Dad was flying back from some business trip in Spain and would pick up the car. Saved them massive taxi fares too, so they were happy all round."

Carrie felt herself begin to shake, trying to think what time Daniel had put her in bed.

He couldn't have gone! Her dad had to be mistaken. Cold fear swept over her as she realized that he hadn't even said goodbye to her. Tears welled into her eyes and she stopped breathing entirely as her lungs felt as though they had collapsed under the constriction of the tightening rubber band.

And then all she could feel was pain inside her chest, all she could hear was a roaring of blood in her ears. There was sudden shouting and then she felt hands on her body, lifting her, moving her, the familiar smell of the leather in her father's car, before darkness swept in and overtook her, leaving nothing but the sound of her own heart beating inside her, letting her know that she was still painfully alive.

Voices collided above her head. She tried to block them out, but they kept intruding and eventually she had to listen.

"It's not normal Helen. Either she's so exhausted from that damn tour or she's had some kind of breakdown. I swear it's that great oaf of a gorilla's fault. She was absolutely fine until I told her about him leaving yesterday. Good riddance to him if you ask me." Jim was sounding very satisfied, though still worried.

Her mother's voice was slightly manic.

"Shh! You idiot. She can probably still hear you, the doctor said she's just in some kind of self-induced faint. And I don't know how you can be so horrible about Daniel. I thought he was a very nice young man. He was always polite to me. I'm going to miss him, and I think that you should realize that Carrie is going to miss him too."

Jim made a strange grumbling noise in his throat and then choked out.

"Miss him! You must be joking. I didn't like him coming round here Helen. God! He practically lived round here that week she was sick. Carrie's far too young to be influenced so much by someone like him. She's got her whole life in front of her and, what with the way he looked at her, I'm certainly not going to pretend to be sorry that he's on the other side of the Atlantic Ocean. I'd prefer it if he were on the other side of the Pacific, just to make sure there were a few more miles between them."

Carrie felt a cool cloth on her forehead and then her mother spoke gently again.

"I'm not disagreeing with you on the fact that she's young, and I want her to do just as well at college as you do. But I think we have to realize that Daniel meant a lot more to Carrie than we thought. I just didn't understand that she felt so strongly about him. We should have seen this coming. I think she's heartbroken."

Jim huffed impatiently.

"Heartbroken? Well if that's all she's had broken by him, then she's damn lucky. I still think she should have a pregnancy test just to make sure. I know he went along to a couple of those concerts during the summer. If he has gone and got her up the duff, at least we can do something about it before it's too late."

Carrie felt her mother get up off the bed. Helen took a long audible breath.

"You can be a miserable bastard when you want to be Jim. It's not anything like that at all. Daniel just wouldn't, I know it…Paul with that Lisa, well that's a different kettle of fish. He seems wilder somehow, still nice but just more of a player, but Lisa is a couple of years older than our Carrie and should know what she is doing, but Daniel's not like Paul. He wouldn't take advantage of her I'm sure. He's old fashioned, somehow more respectful. He hasn't touched her Jim, I know it." She spoke with finality.

But Jim wouldn't leave it.

"Well then, that just goes to prove that he's gay then doesn't it. I mean just look at her. I know she's my daughter but she's absolutely gorgeous, any normal bloke would be all over her. He's definitely queer. I always suspected it."

Helen walked across the room and opened the door for her husband. She stood back and glared at him.

"Get out Jim. You're being utterly ridiculous. And offering backhanded compliments about your daughter doesn't make you right. If you can't say anything nice about the young man, then don't say anything at all. After all, he's not going to be back for at least three years. If he comes home then and they still want to see each other at least by then she'll be over eighteen and there won't be a thing you can do about it."

Carrie heard her father muttering as he walked out of the bedroom. She heard the click as the door closed quietly, then she felt her mother sit on the side of her bed again.

"Carrie love. Can you hear me?" Gentle fingers ran down the side of Carrie's face.

Carrie couldn't deceive her mother and gave a tiny, miserable nod. She opened her swollen eyes to look at her.

"I'm sorry mum." Her voice was just a hoarse whisper. "I didn't mean to spoil everything you'd done for tonight."

Helen leaned over and kissed Carrie's forehead.

"Don't be silly. I should have realized you'd be far too tired. It's all gone in the freezer anyway so don't worry about it. And don't take any notice of your father either. He'd say it about any young man who was interested in you. He's just being over protective.

He doesn't mean all that stuff about Daniel. "

Carrie's heart contracted at the sound of his name and she gave a great gasp of pain. A tear leaked out of one corner of her eye.

"I wasn't going to try and stop him going or anything. I just wanted to say goodbye properly. I love him mum! But I didn't get to tell him. I didn't tell him how I felt at all and it's going to be three years until I can! It's so long. What if he meets someone while he's over there? There's bound to be hundreds of fabulously fit women out there to tempt him. We haven't spent any time together over the summer and I'm going to miss him so much. It won't be the same without him around."

Her mother laughed quietly as she pulled Carrie's hair away from her face.

"No, it won't. It'll feel much more roomy for a start."

Carrie gave a hint of a smile through her tears.

"You should have been around when the whole team got together, then you'd know what crowded really felt like. They're all massive."

Helen smiled in relief.

"Well, I'm glad you can joke about it. But on a more serious note, if you really do love him then you should wait for him. These three years are going to fly by. You're going to be so busy with your 'A' levels and then maybe university, that you wouldn't have much chance to see each other anyway. It's probably best he's thousands of miles away, rather than just a few hundred. At least you know you can't see him."

Carrie sniffed loudly and her mother passed her a tissue.

"I know, I ought to feel happy that he has this fabulous placement, with his best friend, and that this move may make his fortune, but I just don't. Do you know that Paul has asked Lisa to go out there with him? He's only known her a few weeks but can't bear to be apart from her. As soon as he can afford to rent a place for them both she's going. I've known Daniel for years but he didn't ask me to go. He didn't even ask me to wait for him." She sulked miserably before she added. "Maybe I won't have to worry about other women after all. Maybe he really is gay and I should be worrying about all those super fit guys out there." More tears suddenly leaked out.

Helen was silent for a few seconds. Then she shook her head firmly.

"I don't think so Carrie. I didn't get that sort of feeling about him at all. Not that my opinion means much. I think it's just that you're so much younger than Lisa. You know how he feels about having a good education. He probably thought, quite rightly, that you should still be at school. I could see the way he looked at you. It was more than just friends Carrie, and whatever your father thinks, I'm sure he's not gay."

Carrie gave frustrated sigh.

"Then why didn't he say anything to me then. I've been putting it out for months. We've held hands and he has even kissed me on my cheek. He had his hands all over my shoulders and neck after that injury but he never said a thing about wanting me or loving me or even anything about having a quick fumble. The closest he came to saying anything remotely serious was telling me that he was going to miss me." She struggled to sit up.

Helen frowned.

"What injury?" She hadn't listened past those words.

Carrie gulped as she realized she'd let the cat out of the bag, and then she sighed in resignation and decided to come clean.

"I pretended I was sick back in June. That cow Jen and her mates dislocated my shoulder on the last day of the exams. They shut me in the fire doors as I came out of the hall. I made Daniel push it back in place." She rushed on at her mother's horrified expression. "He'd done it before on Paul, but even though he was really gentle, it was horribly painful. I came over all faint and then he was worried that I wouldn't be fit enough for the dance tour. That's why he was here when I said I was sick. He was doing his special physiotherapy on me."

Helen pulled in a sharp breath.

"Carrie! Why on earth didn't you go to hospital? You shouldn't have let him experiment on you. He's not qualified. What if he'd made it worse?"

Carrie shrugged.

"Mum, Daniel had done a first aid course and a sports injury therapy course. He barely touched me at all anyway. He just rolled my joint back into place and gave me instructions on how to keep it flexible, but it doesn't matter now anyway. It's completely healed so he must have done a good job. You would have stopped me going on the tour if we hadn't kept it a secret, which is exactly what Jen wanted. It was all those special exercises of Daniel's that made it right in time."

Helen looked at her daughter's shoulder critically and then shook her head in disbelief.

"I might have known you were up to something. You're never ill. I can't believe I didn't see it. Jim suspected all the time that there was something else going on, but he just jumped to the wrong conclusion and thought that Daniel was trying to get you into bed. I don't think I'm going to tell him he was even half right. He'll be so bloody superior, and I can't believe that Jennifer! What a thing to do! She should be locked up. I hope you reported her to the teachers. She should have been suspended."

Carrie shrugged again.

"She's not going to be at college this year.

Apparently she's given up dancing altogether and is doing something with the local paper. Lisa's mum cut out a small article she'd done about us dancing on the tour and sent it for us to look at. I don't know why she bothered. Jen had the cheek to say that we were "Stiff and un co-ordinated." Load of rubbish of course, but she's still blinded by her jealousy. Do you know she was doing all sorts of stupid stuff after I won the place to back the band. She put jam doughnuts in my shoes, threw chewing gum in my hair and even managed to steal my locker key and fill the thing with foam. I had a detention for that, though Dan did manage to make the caretaker see reason in the end. Half my books were ruined."

Helen's frown deepened.

"Why the little moo! If I ever see her again…"

Carrie shook her head.

"Don't even waste your time mum. It was all so pathetic, really childish. She can't do anything to me now so I'm just going to forget about it. Do you mind if I don't come down tonight, I can't face dad if he's going to be like the Spanish Inquisition. Apart from the Daniel thing, I really am shattered."

Helen stood up and walked towards the door.

"No, that's fine. Stay where you are, I'll bring you up a cup of tea and some sandwiches in a while." She hesitated for a moment and then turned back. "There's always the phone and email you know. You can still keep in touch with Daniel."

Carrie looked hard at her mother.

"He never said anything about that to me. I'll let him be the first to call. If he wants to keep in touch, he knows where I am."

Chapter Seven
Late November 2007

Carrie watched suspiciously as Lisa walked off the dance floor. Her hands were on her hips and she was breathing heavily. She waved her hand in dismissive frustration at Antonio as he looked as if he were about to follow her. She hurried out of the door and Carrie saw her sit on the low wall outside the studio, her head in her hands.

Antonio gave Lisa a hard stare and then turned to the other sweating dancers.

"I don't know what's got into her. She's lost all her stamina. Well, that's not happening to you lot. We're going to step up the training from next week. I'm fitting in an extra hour on Mondays and Fridays. I'm not having any of you lot slacking, we have a load of new routines to work on and I'm going to be doing a lot with your flexibility. We will not be "Stiff and un co-ordinated" ever again. Come on, through the set again!"

There was a general groan from around the room.

Carrie wandered over to the door and watched as Lisa bent over the wall and looked as though she were being sick.

"I'm just going to check on Lisa. She looks as though she's ill." She yelled over the pounding music.

She grabbed up her water from the floor, opened the door and was out of the studio door before Antonio could object.

Carrie stood beside Lisa and put her arm round her shoulder. She didn't look up but shivered in the cool air, retched again and then wiped the back of her hand over her mouth. Carrie handed her the bottle of water.

"When are you going stop trying to cover this up?" She demanded as Lisa swilled water around her mouth and then spat it out in the grass at the other side of the wall.

She looked up, slightly bleary eyed.

"Cover up what exactly?" She dropped her eyes to the pavement as her cheeks suddenly flushed.

Carrie sighed in exasperation.

"For goodness sake Lisa. I may not have much personal experience but I did take sex education lessons and I'm certainly not stupid. You're obviously pregnant. You shouldn't be doing all this dancing! You're either going to kill yourself or the baby or both. Either get rid of it or stop the dancing." She sat on the wall beside her friend.

Lisa's lips trembled for a second and she took another sip of water, then looked at Carrie with tears in her eyes.

"I couldn't get rid of it. I love it already. That night in Birmingham was the best of my life. We just couldn't help ourselves, it wasn't planned so we didn't use anything but I don't regret a second of it. I wanted him so much and I thought he felt the same. I was hoping that he would have said more about me going over there by now. It's been nearly three months and he's only just found a part time job that fits in with the sports training. His trial with the Atlanta Raiders is early next week, so he's hoping that if he is selected he can afford something more then."

Carrie nodded, wishing Lisa would say something about Daniel. She hadn't had any news at all. No phone calls, no emails and no letters.

She had given up waiting and, in desperation, had tried his mobile number on several occasions but it had gone straight to voice mail. It was only later that she remembered that he had left it behind. Now she rang it nearly every evening, just to hear his gorgeously deep voice saying.

"Hi, this is Daniel. Leave your message after the tone and I'll get back to you."

He never did get back to her.

Mostly she just listened to him, but sometimes she whispered.

"I miss you Dan." One night she had even breathed, "I love you Dan," by mistake. At first she had been frantic with worry about it, but then, when she had calmed down, she realized that it didn't matter. He wasn't picking up anyway.

Now, most nights before she went to sleep, she rang his number and whispered, "I love you Daniel." As his recorded voice faded away.

She put her hand over Lisa's and squeezed gently.

"Have you told Paul about the baby?"

Lisa shook her head.

"I can't yet. I don't want to make him have to ask me over. I don't want to feel like I'm a burden, forcing him to have me there."

Carrie sighed.

"I think you should tell him right away. He's going to have to face up to his responsibilities sometime soon and support you both anyway, so he might as well get used to the idea. It will make him focus on this Atlanta trial if he has an incentive. And a baby is a pretty big incentive."

Lisa gave a dismissive shrug.

"Depends on if you want one or not. If he doesn't want me or this baby, he may not try very hard at all. I want him to ask me over before I tell him."

Carrie laughed.

"Well, I should tell him before it shows too much. You may give him a heart attack if you waddle out of the airport with a massive baby belly that he's not expecting."

Lisa laughed back at her as she rubbed her hand gently over her stomach.

"I guess you're right. That's probably not the best way to find out that you're going to be a dad. I'll just have to be brave and tell him the next time he rings." Then she suddenly jumped up off the wall and wrung her hands in panic. "But what if he really doesn't want it or me? What if it was just a one night stand and he says he doesn't want me to go out there?"

Carrie laughed even louder.

"You idiot Lisa. You know he loves you. He rings you two or three times a day. I think he blows his whole spending budget calling you all the time. You both knew what you were doing when you were at that hotel, and he must have wondered if he'd made you pregnant, especially as you didn't use any protection. I expect he was waiting for you to say something last month."

Lisa smiled wistfully.

"He did keep asking me if I was okay." She yawned widely. "I'm going to have to tell Antonio soon as well. There's no way I'll be dancing for the New Year concerts, I can barely keep up now. He'll want to find someone to take my place."

Carrie turned sideways to her.

"How do you feel about giving it all up?"

Lisa shrugged.

"Right at this moment, I'm so knackered and my boobs are so sore, I couldn't care less about it all. We'll just have to see if I can keep fit enough to go back to it afterwards, but if Paul is okay with everything, I won't be worrying about that anyway."

Carrie smiled at her again and then looked back to where she could see the others whirling about inside the studio.

"Does Paul ever say anything about Daniel?"

Lisa grinned.

"I thought you'd never ask! All the time. They are best friends Carrie. They do practically everything together. They're even working in the same bar in the evenings and Daniel's trial for the Raiders is the day before Paul's. You know, I think if only one of them gets a place on the team, I'm sure the other won't do it without them. They're more like brothers than friends." She patted Carrie's hand. "I'm pretty sure you don't have anything to worry about Carrie. Paul says that Daniel keeps himself really quiet. He's not like the rest of the students. He doesn't go out with any of the girls that hang around them all the time."

Carrie sighed again. It wasn't much comfort. Rather than reassure her, it just made her certain that he preferred men to women. She stood up and turned back to the studio as Lisa's phone suddenly rang.

Her trembling hand moved to her pocket and then hesitated. Carrie waited for a second and then encouraged her.

"I bet that's Paul now. Go on, answer it. For goodness sake tell him before it's too late. I'm going back in before Antonio blows a fuse. I'll speak to you afterwards okay?"

Lisa nodded and bent her head to her phone. Carrie heard a few quiet words of their conversation.

"Paul, I need to tell you something, please don't be mad…No! You idiot, stop shouting! I haven't found another boyfriend, just listen will you…"

The doors shut behind Carrie and she joined in with the routine on the edge of the dance floor. She went through the moves as if on automatic pilot, wishing with all her heart that it was her who had had the most wonderful night of her life with the man she loved and that it was she who was pregnant.

She could almost feel Daniel's massive, muscled body clasping her tightly as she danced. She closed her eyes, wondering what their first time together would have been like. She had felt his chest and arms often enough, but the rest of him…She gave a thrilling shiver as she danced, the thoughts spinning around and around in her head, building and then peaking, almost reaching a climax…Then she came back down to earth and opened her eyes as the music suddenly stopped and she heard Antonio's furious yell.

"What the hell do you mean? Pregnant! You have a contract here and you cannot be pregnant Lisa! I forbid it!" His face was purple with rage.

Lisa lifted her chin defiantly.

"I'm leaving Antonio. I don't care about the

contract. I'm going to America. I was just on the phone with Paul and told him about the baby. He says I'm to take the next flight out. If I don't arrive in Atlanta by tomorrow night, he's coming to get me." She was beaming with happiness as she walked to the back of the studio and picked up her duffel bag, then she skipped straight back to Carrie and hugged her hard. "I'll call you as soon as I get there okay. Paul's thrilled. He's going to find somewhere for us today. He says he's just being lazy and not looking hard enough. Life's pretty easy on campus, but he reckons if he and Daniel pool their rent money, they can find somewhere a little out of town with two or even three bedrooms that they can afford between them. We're going to all be living together." Her eyes were shining brightly.

Carrie hugged Lisa back. She was thrilled for her friend, but also as envious of her as she had been of anyone in her entire life. For just one second she thought that she knew exactly how Jennifer Crane had felt when Carrie had won the first dancing audition. But Carrie wasn't going to be spiteful about it.

"Thank goodness, now go and book a flight. You've got all my numbers and my email. Let me know how you're getting on as soon as you can." She let Lisa go and turned back to the still purple Antonio. "Come on Antonio. We'll be fine without her. You still have the rest of us."

Antonio gave a great snort and spoke bitterly.

"Yes, but for how long? As soon as you girls become interested in men, all sense of responsibility goes out of the window. I've seen it happen before. It's an absolute nightmare. You are the best team I have ever had. How am I meant to keep you all together if you all run off and get yourselves pregnant all the time?" He ranted on, sounding close to tears.

James grinned widely and spoke up loudly.

"I don't intend getting pregnant anytime soon Antonio and I'm pretty sure Callum, Joe, Toby and Pete feel the same." Howls of laughter rang round the hall.

Antonio flapped his hands.

"Oh, you lot can mock! It's not funny. I think I'm going to write it into your contracts that you are forbidden to have sex." He ignored the boys as they fell about, laughing hysterically. "Okay Lisa, what's done is done and I wish you well. If you keep the dancing up and ever come back to England, look us up. I'm sure we will be able to find something for someone as talented as you." He held out his hand to her, but she ignored it as she threw her arms around his neck and kissed his cheek.

"Thanks Antonio." She stepped back. "I won't forget you. We'll be back in less than three years. It won't seem like five minutes, so keep me updated on everything you are doing." She gave another quick wave to Carrie and walked out of the doors.

118

Antonio gave a huge sigh.

"This leaves us with hole in our line up and it's going to be too difficult to introduce someone new at this late stage. I think we should alter our positioning and have a look round for a replacement after Christmas." He glanced around at each of them as they all nodded and spaced out again. "Right, Carrie, with one less girl in the crew I'm moving you up a line. Don't forget to go backwards three paces more when you come to the formation. Okay, let's go again. On Four." He started the music up again and Carrie put everything she could into it. It must have been okay as Antonio didn't moan and only corrected her positioning once. Everyone else fitted in around her and the rehearsal came to a close with everyone hitting high fives and promising to do even better the next time.

That night Carrie rang Daniel's phone and said.

"I expect you've heard the news. I'm going to miss her but I'm really happy for Lisa and Paul. She'll be with you tomorrow evening..." She hesitated for a moment and then added quietly. "I wish it was me coming to meet you Daniel. I love you."

Chapter Eight
June 2008

Carrie looped her hair up behind her ear as she bent over her desk, checking her exam paper. She felt a strange sense of de-ja-vu creep over her and she looked up at the clock. There were only a few minutes to go. She sat up straight and looked over to the person next to her.

Craig Bellamy was swinging on the back two legs of his chair. His pens were lying beside his closed paper. He gave a quick grin and then winked when he saw Carrie looking at him. She rolled her eyes and he thumped the two front legs of the chair down again. The girl at the desk in front of him jumped violently and knocked her pens off the table. They dropped noisily to the floor and the invigilator came rushing up to sort out the commotion.

Carrie stuck her hand over her mouth to stop herself from laughing and Craig gave her another huge grin. Then the bell sounded and the man at the end of the hall said.

"Pens down everybody. Please remain seated and silent until all the papers have been collected."

There was a great scraping of chairs as the door was opened and the A.s. level students filed out, beginning to talk and compare notes on questions they had answered.

Craig caught hold of Carrie's arm as they walked through the doors.

"Hey Carrie, how did it go?" His voice was open and friendly, smile firmly in place.

She smiled back.

"Okay, I think. I'm pretty good with history so I should be alright. What about you?"

He grimaced slightly.

"Probably scraped it. I always get the different treaties mixed up, but anyway all over now until our finals next year. What are you doing tonight? As that was the last exam until next year, we should go and celebrate."

Carrie smiled at him, but shook her head.

"I can't tonight Craig. I'm waiting in to hear news of my friend Lisa. She's having a baby. She went to America with her boyfriend Paul, so there's no way I can visit her. You probably remember him. He was in the rugby team here last year. Paul Edmonds?" She waited until he nodded. "He won a placement in Atlanta. Lisa's one of my old dancing friends but she's obviously given it all up while having Paul's baby. It's due any day now and I want to be there when she rings me. We've set up a web-cam link so she can show me her baby as soon as it's born. Paul is over the moon about it."

Craig looked a little revolted, but more disappointed.

121

"Blimey! He's young to be a father! Oh well, he must have known what he was doing. I suppose it's really nice for you and your friend, but won't having babies have an effect on a dancing career? Is she getting back into it afterwards?"

Carrie shrugged.

"I don't know if it's that easy. She said that she might try some teaching, or maybe choreography but then there's all the hassle of child care. I'm not sure I'd want to leave my baby with anyone else." She thought about this for a moment and then looked back up at Craig. He had said something to her.

"…What about another time then?" He was steering her towards the entrance doors, but he caught hold of her arm again before they went any further and pulled her over to a long bank of lockers. He looked up quickly to see if there was anyone around and then spoke quickly.

"Look Carrie, I've been meaning to ask you for a while. I want you to come out with me. You know, not just on a date, but really go out together. I've liked you for ages." He puffed out a great breath of pent up air.

Carrie looked into his blue, hopeful eyes. He was lovely looking, but she just couldn't feel that flipping sensation. She willed it to start, furious with herself when it didn't. It was nine months since she had seen Daniel. *She should go out with Craig!* She told herself. *He is a really nice guy. Caring and clever. And here!*

She hesitated for a moment and saw Craig's face fall a little. He was waiting for her response. She spoke quietly.

"Maybe just for a coffee. I don't really date. I'm far too busy with the dancing."

Craig's worried expression brightened immediately as he realized that she wasn't giving him the complete brush off.

"Great! A coffee is great. I don't mind that, who knows, you may just enjoy it and want to come out with me some more." His enthusiasm was infectious.

She laughed.

"You never know, but seriously Craig, I really don't date. I'm on tour again this summer, and going by last year's schedule I won't have time to see you at all."

He turned away from her for a moment and fished a key out of his jeans pocket. He stuck it in one of the lockers.

"That's okay, having a coffee with you before you go will be nice. Perhaps we can pick up again in September."

Carrie was about to nod when he opened the locker door. He rooted around for something and then pulled a book out from right at the bottom. A cloud of bright pink dust spilled out with the book and Craig shook it, sending pink dust motes everywhere.

"Sorry." He said as she brushed the colour from

her arm. "It's a damn nuisance. There's been something in here all year that just won't go away. I didn't notice it at first, but now it's falling off the inside of the locker walls. It's obviously dried on and flaking away when my books brush against it. I've asked to change lockers but there aren't any other ones available." He put another book into his bag and shut the locker door.

Carrie noticed the number on the outside. It was her old locker from the previous year. She had given it up herself when she had become fed up with the dried out pink foam still lingering in the locker's metal seams.

For a moment she thought she was going to laugh, but as she thought of how Daniel had helped her with the mess, her heart began to beat faster and she suddenly found it hard to breathe.

Craig looked down at her as she gasped in a gulp of air. Carrie's eyes wandered up to his face. He was tall and good looking, but nowhere near the size of Daniel or as handsome. His hair was dark but it wasn't dark like Daniel's, his eyes were blue but not as intense as Daniel's, his voice wasn't deep like Daniel's. She began to choke. Craig wasn't Daniel.

He was looking at her quizzically.

"Are you okay? You don't think that stuff has given you some kind of asthma attack do you?"

Carrie shook her head.

"No." She coughed to cover the strangled tone of her voice. She was thinking of Daniel the year before, as he had helped her with the goo. His beautiful dark hair, still damp from the shower, his straight, white teeth, his deep blue eyes and soft voice. She remembered his huge hands mopping out the pink foam and the waft of aftershave as he had leaned over her, trying and failing to pull the silly string from her hair. She sighed deeply.

"This used to be my locker Craig. Some idiot nicked my key and sprayed silly foam inside it half way through the term last year. It was everywhere. Daniel Lewis helped me clear it up. Obviously we made a terrible job of it. Sorry." She felt a strange jolt in her stomach as she realized that she had been the one to suggest going out for a coffee with Craig. She looked back at his still hopeful face. Now she had thought of Daniel, it seemed a ridiculous thing to do. She didn't want to go out with Craig. She didn't want to go out with anyone but Daniel, however hopeless it was.

Craig was brushing more pink powder from his books. He looked sideways at her.

"You mean that great lump of a bloke who now plays football out in America with that Paul? It was funny about him. I always thought he had an eye for you, and at one point I thought it was him doing all that bullying stuff just to get himself noticed by you. I don't suppose he needs to now though. You can't help noticing him or his mate. They must be raking it in with that massive Atlanta contract. Ten million Dollars for his first year! Incredible!"

Carrie opened her eyes wide at the two new bits of information.

She had never suspected Daniel of sabotaging her at school. He had been the one who was always around to clear up afterwards. Craig must have made a mistake. And Lisa had certainly failed to mention ten million dollars in their last phone call. If Daniel was earning that much, then Paul probably was too. No wonder she hadn't said anything about going back to dancing. She obviously didn't need to. Carrie turned away from Craig suddenly. She was going to have to go home and email Lisa immediately. She had to know what was going on.

"I'll see you around Craig. I'll let you know when Lisa has had her baby, and then I'll see if I have time for that drink when I'm back from the tour, okay?" Carrie jogged out of the door feeling a little bit bad. There was no way she was going to go out with Craig, but at least she had bought herself some time. Maybe he wouldn't be quite so interested in her by the end of the summer.

She walked home quickly and was surprised to see a small crowd gathered around her gate. She was about to push her way through when her ex-friend

126

Jennifer Crane stepped over to her. Carrie hadn't seen her in almost a year and she wasn't that keen on renewing the acquaintance now. She looked down and noticed that Jennifer held a notebook in her hand and that she was smiling over sweetly.

"Hey Carrie! It's been a while. Finished your exams?" She followed Carrie's gaze and then carried on without waiting for a response. "I'm working for the Harrow Gazette now and I was wondering if you would like to comment on your friend Daniel Lewis's contract with the Atlanta Raiders. Ten million Dollars in the first year! You must have something to say."

Carrie stared at Jennifer and tried to walk round her. Jennifer skipped sideways and blocked her path.

"No, I've nothing to say." Carrie gritted her teeth as the young woman refused to move out of her way. Jennifer smiled even more widely.

"Oh! I see, you're jealous of his success." Jennifer scribbled something on the notepad. "Well, I can understand that, it must be galling to be famous before him, but still only pull in peanuts by comparison. But then dancing has never been a very lucrative career. Can you tell us about your relationship with him? I understood that you were pretty close at one time. Last summer, the neighbours round here tell me, you spent a lot of time together. Can you give me an angle on that? What does it feel like to be jilted for the high life in America?"

Carrie gawped at the horrible woman in front of her, about to give her piece of her mind, but then she noticed the notebook with pencil still poised.

"I'm not famous Jen! And I don't want to be, not if it means having you staking out my home. And no, I don't have anything else to say about my relationship with my friend Daniel either. Can I get to my house Jen? I've had my last A. s. today and I'm shattered. I really don't want to talk to you." She shoved past and Jennifer staggered backwards, winking at her camera man as she made a big thing of being pushed out of the way.

"There's no need to be such a Prima Donna, Carrie Denton. You changed so much after being handed that dancing contract. The high life has really gone to your head. Maybe it'll do you good to be brought down a peg or two. It might teach you some manners." Jennifer shouted at Carrie's retreating back.

Carrie ignored her and opened the front door. Her mother called out as she did every day.

"That you Carrie?"

"Yes mum. What are all those people doing at the gate and why is the local paper suddenly so interested in Daniel?" She thumped her bag down in the hall and walked through to the kitchen.

Helen was pouring a glass of freshly made lemonade. She handed it to Carrie.

"Stupid old bag has been out there half the day.

There was a big headline on the news because Daniel scored the winning touchdown in the final seconds of the American football finals. Paul had passed him the ball from way back up the pitch. He was through the defence like they didn't exist and was off like a rocket. There was no way anyone was going to catch him. Even I have to admit that it was quite exciting. You know, English men winning for the Americans and all that. He and Paul were pictured being carried off the pitch on the team members' shoulders. The crowd were going mad! Apparently they've been offered a huge contract on the back of it. I was looking at it the press conference at lunch time."

Carrie finished the lemonade and rinsed the glass in the sink.

"Paul shouldn't be playing. Lisa is about to have his baby, he should be with her." Her tone was indignant.

Helen laughed.

"I don't think what I was watching was live and in any case I don't suppose he's left her unattended Carrie. She probably has the best care money can buy. It really won't matter if he's there or not and this was a really important game. You can hardly blame him."

"That's not the point." Carrie retorted as she slipped off her jacket. "A husband should want to be with his wife at a time like this. It's really important for the mother and the baby. If he's going to go gallivanting about with this football lark, why did he ask her to go over there? He won't have time to help look after the baby."

Helen gave a derisive snort.

"You must be living in cloud-cuckoo-land if you think anyone is going to give up the chance of ten million dollars. I know I wouldn't. They'll work it out Carrie, after all he married her as soon as she arrived over there. He didn't have to do that. It's just how Paul is, now if it had been Daniel with the very expectant wife, well, I think he might even have turned down the contract. He seems to be a little old fashioned. I'm surprised your dad didn't like him more."

Carrie rolled her eyes.

"Don't talk to me about dad. He keeps on going on about this summer season tour and how important it is. I'm completely knackered mum. I'm seventeen and done in. I've worked constantly since last April and I haven't a thing to show for it except sore muscles and a bank balance that I can't touch until I'm eighteen. I need a holiday." She slumped down into a chair and laid her head on the kitchen table.

Helen sat down with her.

"Come on Carrie love, it's not like you to be down. Why don't you go and have a chat to Lisa? If she's not in hospital that is. She normally makes you feel better."

Carrie blinked into her folded arms.

"That's only because she tells me what Dan's been up to. Oh God! I bet dad goes completely the other way about Dan now. He'll probably want to be his best friend and I bet he moans about me not going out with him after all." She dragged herself out of the chair.

Her mum laughed.

"Well it serves him right that you're not with Daniel. It'll teach Jim not to be so judgmental. Now go on, go and see if Lisa has any news about the baby."

Carrie trudged up the stairs. She looked out of the landing window as she heard the honking of a horn. Her father was trying to manoeuvre past the crowd outside the gate. His expression was livid as Jennifer tried to shove a microphone through the car window. Carrie slid into her bedroom and shut the door firmly. She dumped her bag on her desk and fired up the computer.

Lisa was already on line even though it must have been late in the evening.

"Hey Carrie, it's good to see you. I guessed you would be home about now. I'm so bored stuck here. Paul wouldn't let me go to the finals. He's still out after the game and he's organized the most military midwife you could imagine. I'm calling her Attila. She tells me what to do all the time. She has a list of things that have to be done exactly on time every day or she's getting the doctor out to me. Do you have any idea how difficult it is to poo to order?" She was obviously exasperated.

Carrie laughed out loud, feeling instantly happier.

"No, can't say that I have ever been asked to 'poo' on demand. Sounds terrible. I did my last exam today. I can't believe it's a whole year since I dislocated my shoulder. Things have moved on so fast."

Lisa nodded in agreement.

"You're telling me. I could never have imagined being in this state this time last year. I must have been mad!"

Carrie could see Lisa wincing as she rubbed her huge stomach.

"Are you very uncomfortable? You look ready to pop."

Lisa pulled a pained face.

"I think it's because it's so close. I feel as tight as a drum, and it hurts like hell every so often, but I'm not saying anything to Attila because she'll have her hand up my skirt in an instant. She's already moaning because I'm a few days late and she thinks the baby is too big for me, but it was fine on the last scan. She keeps on wanting to have a look "up there" and see if I'm dilating."

Carrie was horrified.

"Is the baby too big for you? Paul is huge, so it

could be, I suppose…Lisa!" She shouted as her friend suddenly cried out and doubled over. "Lisa, get Attila now." Carrie yelled and jumped up from her chair as she heard Lisa gasping into the webcam. After a few moments her head came up again. Carrie could see a film of sweat on her friend's upper lip.

Lisa moaned into the camera.

"God! That was a bad one. The contractions are becoming harder to bear, but I can't call Attila. I told her to go home after she made me shower for the third time today. Something about a warm water stimulus. I couldn't stand all the fuss and told her to go away as I felt fine then. She's forgotten her phone, it's here on the desk." Lisa was gasping again as another contraction gripped her.

Carrie ran to the door and called her mother.

"Mum! Lisa is on line and I think she's having her baby. Right now. She's on her own mum, the midwife has gone home." Her voice was panicked.

Helen stood for a moment, her head poking out of the lounge door as she stared up at Carrie and then she pounded up the stairs. She took one look at Lisa's image on the screen and sat down in front of the computer. She spoke quickly.

"Call nine one one honey. Stay on line here and talk to us until they arrive okay." Helen made herself comfortable in Carrie's chair and watched while Lisa gave breathless instructions to the operator. "While you're waiting we can do some breathing exercises to help with the pain." Helen encouraged. "…If I can remember any of them that is." She added a little doubtfully.

Carrie leaned over her mother's shoulder and spoke into the webcam.

"How about doing those exercises that Dan showed me? You don't even have to get out of the chair Lisa. They were very relaxing and I can't see how they would hurt. I'll do them with you. Copy me while I talk you through it all."

Lisa took a couple of breaths and nodded into the camera. Helen angled the viewfinder towards Carrie. She sat on the floor and raised her hands above her head.

"Now breathe deeply, let your arms fall to your sides and then raise them gently again. Lift your ribcage and then breathe out slowly. Control your breath...And breathe out and relax." Carrie's voice was calm, even Helen copied her and felt a deep sense of release come over her whole body. Carrie kept on with the instructions, only stopping when the pain was obviously too great for Lisa to concentrate, and then she talked to her through the contraction, starting the instructions again as soon as Lisa was able to unclamp her teeth.

It was only as Helen looked at her watch for the fifth time that Carrie realized that more than a few minutes had passed. It was nearer half an hour.

Carrie picked up on the worried look on her mother's face. She spoke to Lisa again.

"I think you need to stand if you can Lisa. Are you able to get to the window and see if the medics are coming? They seem to have been a long while."

Lisa moved slowly and groaned as she hung onto the curtains.

"Nothing." She managed to gasp after looking out of the window. It was obviously dark outside. "I should be able to see them from miles away. We're a bit remote out here. We moved because of all the attention Paul and Dan were attracting. It was getting scary with all the fans hanging around all day. We've kept this place hushed up, and we don't have any nosey neighbours either." She dropped the curtain again.

Helen moved swiftly out of the chair. She grabbed up Carrie's mobile and rang nine, nine, nine. She explained the situation rapidly to the operator and gave Lisa's address in Atlanta, then she put the phone down again as Carrie continued with the exercises. Lisa's breathing was becoming deeper and she suddenly let out a huge groan.

"Oh God! I think my water's just broke, they've gone everywhere, what do I do now?" Lisa was beginning to panic.

Carrie was almost frantic. She was so glad her mother was with her.

Helen took over.

"You need to lay down Lisa love. If your waters have gone all at once, the cord may slip around your baby's neck. Are you near a bed?"

Lisa shook her head as the sweat dripped from her brow.

"Office." She panted and gritted her teeth again, then when the pain was over she pulled the camera off the desk and slipped to the floor. She groaned as another contraction caught her and then she was crying out in agony.

Helen shouted over her cries.

"Don't push too hard Lisa, let the baby come down slowly, can you reach down and see if you can feel its head yet?"

Carrie stared at the web-cam, horrified as Lisa somehow managed to pull herself forwards. She wriggled around for a moment as she removed her underwear, then she lifted her skirt and put her hand between her legs. She nodded and gasped out.

"I can feel the top, but it's not right out." She flopped back onto the floor panting breathlessly.

Helen spoke slowly and clearly.

"Okay, now on the next contraction, try and pant not push. We have to wait for the baby's head to come through gently. Push as little as possible. The baby's head needs to come out slowly or you'll tear. And you need to check the cord straight away. If it's around his neck, un-loop it immediately, okay honey? I know it's hard but you have to do this. Do you understand?" Carrie saw Lisa nod once before her face scrunched up and she began pushing hard.

"No!" Carrie shouted at once. "Mum said gently. Breathe with me Lisa and push down slowly." They could see Lisa trying to calm herself and then she let out a great scream just as a door burst open behind her.

Paul came charging through into the office. He took one look into the webcam, then immediately knelt down between Lisa's spread legs and caught the baby in his huge hands just as it slipped out of his wife's body.

The next few minutes were pandemonium. Helen was shouting for Paul to check that the cord was free and that the baby was breathing. There was an anxious moment until Paul tapped his tiny son on his back. The baby gave a great shuddering gasp, then began to yell lustily.

Lisa was crying, Paul was crying, Helen and Carrie were crying. Paul was on still his knees with his wife and new baby son, holding the tiny squalling thing to his chest and kissing Lisa madly, then he bent forwards and kissed the webcam, not caring that his tears were streaming onto the lens.

"Thank you, thank you, thank you. Carrie, Helen, I don't know what to say." He was stammering wildly, barely in control of himself.

Helen and Carrie were wiping their eyes. Helen managed to splutter.

"It's not over yet Paul. You need to keep the baby warm, can you wrap him in something, and the placenta needs to be delivered too. Lisa's going to have another contraction in about ten minutes and you'll have to pull on the cord to help it out."

Paul nodded as he immediately ripped off his huge t-shirt and wrapped his baby snugly in it.

"I don't think I'll have to worry. I can hear the ambulance. Thank God I came home instead of staying out celebrating our win. I can't thank you two enough. We were going to ask Carrie anyway, but Helen, you have to be a godmother too now. I don't know what Lisa would have done without both of you." His happiness was obvious.

He placed the baby in Lisa's arms and wiped the tear stained webcam before continuing.

"I'm going to let the medics in. Stay on line and talk to Lisa while I do some phoning round. I must let Dan know he's a Godfather. He's gonna be so excited."

Carrie suddenly leaned forwards and asked.

"Is Daniel with you now? I'd love to have a word if he's about."

Paul looked into the screen. He was suddenly serious.

"I'm sorry Carrie. I've asked him loads of times

before to talk to you, but he just won't. He even leaves the house if Lisa is on the line to you. He says that you know why he can't and he won't break his word. I can't force him…Oh, the door-bell just went, talk to Lisa for a moment while I get it."

He was gone, but Carrie couldn't speak to Lisa. She moved to the side of the camera and let her mother gush as Lisa held up her new baby for them to look at. The little lad's cheeks were red and blotchy but he looked a good size. Then it was all bustle again as paramedics came crowding into the room surrounding Lisa and her baby, before the screen became fuzzy and the webcam was suddenly shut off.

Carrie sat down on the end of her bed, completely stunned by Paul's words, as her mother swivelled the chair towards her.

"My Goodness that was a close one. What a relief Paul came in just in time. Poor Lisa must have been frantic…So what pact did you make with Daniel that he can't break and come and speak to you? Especially at a moment like this. You're both going to be Godparents after all."

Carrie shook her head in confusion.

"I have absolutely no idea. I didn't agree anything with him. The last time I saw him he just stuffed his face with food like it was going out of fashion and then after some coffee, he left. He didn't really say anything." She wasn't going to give her mother the details of her sleeping on his lap on the hotel terrace, especially as her father was now standing at the door. He was shifting uncomfortably from foot to foot. He had heard all of the last part of the conversation.

He coughed noisily before he spoke.

"That sounded awful, are you sure she was alright?"

Helen looked at Jim suspiciously for a moment and then answered.

"Yes, I think everything is fine and she has all the right medical care now. I'm pretty sure they won't even take her to hospital. Once the baby is born and he looked pretty healthy, there's not much anyone else can do. Thank goodness you mailed her right then Carrie. It would have been horrendous if she had been on her own. Those exercises of Daniel's were fantastic. He ought to set up places teaching them. Talk about a stress buster." She gave a relieved sigh.

Jim suddenly spluttered.

"Yes, it seems he might have been better than I thought at a few things, still I'm glad he's not around here anymore. Those sort of fancy exercise plans are just what the Americans love and now it won't matter if he is gay or not. He's famous after that touchdown today. You can bet your life they'll offer him just about anything to try and keep him there. He wouldn't have wanted to come back to this sleepy part of Harrow anyway so I hope you didn't make some silly plan that you think he's going to be true to you Carrie, because if you did, you can kiss it goodbye now. I can tell his type a mile off, ten million dollars is a lot of money and I bet they offer him more later on. Gay or not he'll have half the population after him and he won't be interested in you anymore, so I hope you're not still holding a torch for him."

Carrie shot up from the bed, she was suddenly so furious with him that she felt as though she was going to explode.

"Get out Dad! If you value your life and my sanity, get out of my room. I don't want to hear another word against Daniel, ever. Do you have that clear? I've put up with your prejudices for over a year now and I'm not taking it any longer." She started pushing the door of her room closed, but her father pushed back so that her mother could get out. Carrie ranted at the two of them. "I don't know what's going on with him and I don't know what Paul was talking about either. I haven't made any pact or any promises, but I'll tell you now dad, if he does ever come back and says he wants to see me, gay or not, I'm going to be right here waiting for him. I won't go out with another man until I know that it's completely hopeless. I love Daniel more than anything in this world and I'm as jealous as hell of Lisa! I'd love to have Daniel's baby any time he wants. He only has to ask!" She slammed the door hard

141

as she heard her father draw in a shocked breath, and fell back onto her bed.

She looked over at the camera briefly and saw that it was still angled slightly downwards. She sat back upright, tilted it upwards again and wondered whether to call Lisa back. She noticed that her hands were shaking slightly as her fingers hovered over the keyboard. She hesitated for a moment and then clicked the webcam off. She didn't want to disturb Lisa right after she had given birth and she certainly didn't want to hear how perfect everything was in their wonderful lives. She just wanted to curl up into a ball and die.

But then she saw her bag sitting by the computer. She grabbed it up and rummaged for her phone. She dialled Daniel's mobile number and listened to his voice. She didn't know whether to leave a message after what Paul had just told her, but then as the tone finished, she cleared her throat and said as cheerfully as she was able.

"Hey! Well, that was all a bit hectic but I think mother and baby are fine now. Thank goodness my mum was here. At least one of us had some idea of what to do...I love you fellow godparent."

Chapter Nine
December 2008

The studio was cold. Carrie was the first to arrive and Antonio was keen to get started.

"We have a new set to learn. Joanne is shaping up well Carrie but I expect you to lead for a while longer."

Carrie nodded and started warming up. She had told Antonio she was moving on before the next summer season of festivals. She had auditioned for and been offered a job on a world tour with one of the most famous singers around and she wasn't going to have time to do the festival season. She had been lucky that Milana had agreed to her finishing her 'A' levels in June before she joined the rest of the dancers in Madrid for the first leg of the tour.

Carrie's father was sick with worry about it. He wanted her to go to university after her exams, but Carrie wanted a gap year before she started on a sports injury and physiotherapy degree. He'd put as many objections forward as possible to the trip, but Carrie had been adamant. Since the row after Lisa's baby was born, things had been difficult at home and Carrie saw the tour as a way of putting some distance between them, without actually falling out permanently.

Jim kept a running update on Daniel, desperate, Carrie suspected, to catch him with some cheer leader or actress, but so far the worst that he had discovered was that Daniel liked to go fishing with Paul in his spare time. It had come up on a sky sports programme and Jim hated fishing. He had been about to comment on the fact that Daniel rarely did anything without Paul, when he had caught his wife's furious glare from across the dinner table. He changed the subject rapidly.

Carrie kept up with her gorgeous godson's progress via the internet. Earlier that evening he had been waving a chubby little fist madly at her and cooing "Ca, Ca" delightedly. Carrie had smiled and waved back at him and then she goodnight kissed the webcam just before a very proud Paul whisked his son away to bed, leaving Carrie to say goodbye to Lisa. She had shut down the internet link and had run to the dance studio.

When she had first seen the advertisement for dancers for Milana's tour, she hadn't even considered it as a possibility, but then the auditions began, and she thought why not give it a try. She didn't want to be doing festivals every summer for the rest of her dancing life. Milana's tour was being done in two parts with a long break over the Christmas period, and finishing at the start of the festival season the following year. It was a punishing schedule, with them moving every few days across the whole of Europe, Africa and Asia. She would just have time to consider what to do about her university placement before the following September.

At least the tour would keep her busy until Daniel came home. Her heart sank as she thought of the last news article about the Raiders. Daniel was now Captain of the team and going from strength to strength. His university degree was apparently going superbly and he was about to open a sports injury clinic in Atlanta. He had been picked up by the advertising agencies and there were rumours of him being cast in films. He was earning a fortune.

It was no longer about when he came home. It was if he came home. Carrie sometimes thought her father was probably right. If Daniel had wanted to speak or get in contact with her, he would have done it a long time before now, but he was continuing with the silent treatment. She tried not to think about it as she stretched her hamstrings.

Callum walked into the studio. He high-fived Carrie and dumped his stuff at the back of the room. He pulled his jumper over his head and his undershirt rode up with it. Carrie noticed his flat rack of a stomach and sighed deeply as she thought of what Daniel's might look like.

Callum looked up at the sound. He grinned wickedly at her as he noticed the direction of her eyes.

"Like what you see babe?" He stood preening

himself, turning this way and that so she had an all-round view of his midriff. It wasn't the first time she had seen his stomach and as stomachs went it was pretty good, but it didn't attract her at all.

She shrugged disinterestedly.

"It's as good as any other I suppose. I've seen worse, but I've also seen a lot better. Some blokes have superb stomachs." She couldn't remember who's might have been better, but she immediately thought that Daniel's must be perfect, not that she had ever seen it in the flesh, well, not since the swimming gala at primary school when he had been about eight or nine.

Callum pulled his shirt down quickly, obviously insulted.

"Oh really, though why I care I don't know. I'd heard that you weren't interested in men. I thought it was the girls you preferred."

Carrie laughed out loud, wondering why he thought she might be a lesbian. She couldn't remember ever having given anyone that impression. She thought she ought to make her position on the subject plain.

"Girls? Are you mad! I don't know where you got that from Cal. I definitely like blokes, especially ones with ripped abs and a stomach with a sexy triangle of hair that points down over his navel, you know, towards his…" She indicated downwards with her finger and waggled her eyebrows suggestively.

"Carrie Denton!" Antonio bellowed. "You can

leave that kind of talk outside the studio and Callum, keep it covered up for goodness sake. We have to expose enough flesh when we are on stage, we really don't need to see any more of it in here." He huffed as he turned back to the stereo.

Carrie walked over to Callum and then bobbed down as she spoke.

"Who told you I prefer women?" She didn't look him in the eye, but pretended to be retying her trainer.

Callum shrugged as he bent to tie his own trainers.

"I suppose we all just assumed it. You don't go out with anyone and I know you've been asked. Toby's brother Craig said you shot him right down in flames last summer. You were supposed to be going out with him and then called it all off. You can't blame us if we talk Carrie."

Carrie stood up quickly. She was completely stunned as she thought back to the conversation she'd had with Craig Bellamy.

"I didn't even know Craig was Toby's brother, and I didn't call it off. I never said I'd go out with him anyway. I agreed to go out for a coffee after we'd done the summer tour, but he had asked Leanne Farnsworth to go out with him by then and I certainly wasn't going to butt in. What a cheek!"

James, Joe, Toby and Pete suddenly came in through the door together. They were all laughing at something one of them had said.

Callum beckoned them over. He spoke far too loudly, over the top of their laughter.

"Hey you lot, listen up, we've got everything wrong. Carrie's not batting for the other team!" He nodded at Toby. "Your big brother Craig was telling us squibbers. Apparently she likes blokes with hairy bellies!"

Pete grinned at Carrie, immediately lifting his shirt over his head, exposing a chest and stomach covered in thick, black hair.

"Great!" He yelled enthusiastically. "I've fancied you for ages. Will you come out with me Carrie? I only get this lot waxed when we are on stage. The rest of the time I'm like coconut matting."

Carrie blushed furiously.

"Eweh!" She grimaced rather disgustedly, but then her eyes widened in admiration. "Wow! You wax that lot! And I thought having my legs done was bad! You're braver than I thought. Must be agony."

Pete puffed out his hairy chest proudly as he strutted around Carrie.

"It's okay, I'm tough, I can take it. So what do you say, is it good enough?" He pointed down at the hair. "Are you going to come out with me?"

Carrie shook her head and held up her hands.

"Sorry, Thanks, but no thanks. I know you too well to go out with you. Any of you!" She added quickly and backed away as James stepped forwards about to lift his shirt too.

Antonio was flapping again.

"Gentlemen! For goodness sake stop it. Put all that disgusting body hair away immediately and leave the poor girl alone. We're not going to have her here for much longer so let's make the time as pleasant as possible. I don't want to hear anything more about chests or stomachs, hairy or otherwise, now come on, get warmed up or I'm going to have to put on the heating and you know that comes out of the wages for the company, so let's make the heat ourselves eh?"

They all ambled onto the dance floor and started to warm up as the rest of the crew arrived.

Four hours later Antonio nodded his head, satisfied at last.

"Another rehearsal on Friday and then we are ready to roll. I've sorted out the new contracts and we all have a bit of a rise, plus a small bonus for doing all the publicity work for the band as well." He waved down the whoops. "Carrie, now that you are eighteen you'll have to let me know if you want to change any banking arrangements, but just for this week I've done the traditional thing and given you your first wages in cash. The rest of you will have the money put into your accounts as usual. Is that okay with everyone?"

Carrie was looking forward to having her first

pay packet that she could spend. Until now any wages had gone into a savings account and while it was nice to see a decent amount piling up she was desperate to go and splash some cash. Maybe she would have some make-up or a new outfit for over Christmas, or she might take some more driving lessons and actually pass her test this time.

That she had failed the last one miserably, back in the summer, was purely the fault of Daniel Lewis.

The driving examiner had made her drive past a huge advertising hoarding in town and she had unexpectedly seen a larger than life size picture of Daniel smiling down at her. He looked fit, tanned and toned, his dark hair tousled, his blue eyes sparkling and his smile wide. He held a bottle of some famous, nutrient giving, mineral water in one hand and an equally fit, tanned and toned and obviously nutrient loving woman in the other.

Carrie had gritted her teeth and seethed with envy as the advertisement had grabbed her attention. Her foot had suddenly caught on the brake and the accelerator at the same time and the car had lurched all over the road, coming to a grinding halt as she completely forgot about the clutch.

That night she had left an annoyed message on Daniel's phone.

"So! Sabotaging my driving test eh! I will be

150

talking to you about that one when you get home and you had better have some damned good excuse for what you have in your hand, and I don't mean the hand holding the bottle! Never the less," she had added primly. "I still love you Dan."

She had decided not to take another test until the advertisement was removed and only last week she had seen that Daniel was now covered with a goofy looking child playing with an extra soft toilet roll. She thought that it was probably safe for her to drive past that.

She looked up as she realized that she had missed something that Antonio had said. He rolled his eyes as Carrie looked confused.

"For goodness sake Carrie, keep up. Right after the Christmas shows I've managed to get us a brilliant gig. It pays well and just for once it's something fairly local. The American football teams are coming over to showcase their sport in late February. They will be playing until the second week in March. We've been asked to be the cheer team for the games played at Wembley. It's a good gig, a two week slot and all the games are in the evening so they shouldn't clash with either school or college."

Carrie felt heat spreading through her body.

"Wh..what teams are coming?" She stammered slightly.

Antonio glared at her.

"How the devil should I know. I do know those local two lads are coming over with their team. There's been something about them in the Gazette. Beyond that I don't have a clue. All I've been told is that they want us for all the games. We're going to split into two groups, one for each team. Here are the dates and times of the rehearsal schedules and games." He handed out slips of paper.

Carrie looked down at hers. She could barely see the rest of the fixture list as the name "Atlanta Raiders" leapt off the page at her. And then the dates came into view. She started hyperventilating as she realized that some of them clashed with the world tour rehearsals.

"I won't be able to do it Antonio. I will be revising for my 'A' levels and rehearsing for Milana's show." She handed him back the slip of paper.

Antonio pushed it back into her hand.

"I already checked and these games are all evenings. If we can all make the rest, the two you can't do due to commitments with Milana, can be covered by the rest of us. Don't you want to see your boyfriend in action?" He winked at her.

Carrie felt her face turn bright red.

"I don't have a boyfriend! Daniel is just my friend and he won't want to see me prancing about in a cheer kit anyway. I'll do the others but I'm not doing the Atlanta Raiders matches Antonio. If you won't accept my decision, then I won't do any of them!" She was suddenly shouting, tears streaming down her face. She turned away from the rest of the group as they stared incredulously at her outburst, then she grabbed up her bag and made for the door.

Antonio ran after her.

"Carrie!" He called as he ran. He caught up with her and matched her pace. "What's this all about? I thought you would be pleased about it. After that woman wrote that article back in the summer about the two of you splitting up, I thought it would give you the chance to get back together. I thought it would be so romantic if you met up again just before your world tour. I really fought to get you lot this gig."

Carrie stopped and turned on him. Antonio skidded to a halt in front of her. She took the handkerchief that Antonio thrust at her and dabbed at her eyes.

"That article was a load of rubbish, written by a twisted old cow who only did it because I won this contract with you and she didn't. What she wrote wasn't the truth. I wasn't going out with him at all, so I can't have been jilted. I don't even know what the truth is, except that I love him. I can't just turn up at one of his games and expect him to fall all over me. He's not like that." Carrie knew she was making a hash of explaining, but she didn't know how to explain anyway.

Antonio stared down at her.

"But if you love him, why not try and win him back? I don't understand, surely this is a perfect opportunity for both of you."

Carrie shook her head.

"You're not listening Antonio. He doesn't want to see me. I'm in contact with Lisa all the time. Daniel lives with her and Paul and little Tommy. She lets me know what he's up to, but he never speaks to me. He doesn't want to speak to me. I don't know what I've done wrong, but I have to leave it up to him. Paul says he's sure everything is going to turn out fine, I just have to keep to our agreement, but I don't know what he's talking about. I've tried to explain to Paul, but it just goes over his head. He's so wrapped up in becoming a dad, nothing else is as important to him."

Antonio frowned.

"You made some kind of agreement with this Daniel? To do what precisely?"

She sighed, Antonio still wasn't listening.

"I don't know, I never agreed to anything but it must be something to do with not contacting him until his three years are up. What else could it be? It's partly why I want to go away for the next year. I can't stay here after my 'A' levels just hoping he's going to turn up. He's obviously made some kind of commitment to the team that he can't break. He's very loyal like that."

Antonio rubbed his temples.

"You young people are so complicated these

days. I'm so glad I just stick to dancing. It's so much easier than trying to figure out relationships. Look, I'm going back in. I'm not going to hold you to these events Carrie, but you should think seriously before giving them up. They would look excellent on your C.V."

Carrie shrugged.

"Milana's world tour is going to look excellent on my C.V. too Antonio. I'd really rather not do these football things if I don't have to."

Antonio nodded.

"Okay, fine, do what you like. I won't force you to do any of them if you don't feel like it." He turned back to the studio and wandered inside.

Carrie walked along the pavement towards her home. She shivered as the cold air chilled her through her tracksuit. She felt almost angry with Lisa for not warning her that the teams were coming. She was going to have to pull her up on it when they next spoke. It wasn't fair that she found out things like this through a third party.

She quickened her step as it began to drizzle, not wanting to get soaked through. Her mind was turning over and over at the thoughts of missing Daniel on purpose, but then she felt it must be the right decision. He could choose to speak to her any time, but Lisa had taken to calling her when Daniel would be at college or football anyway, so there was no opportunity of even seeing him accidentally.

She played around with different scenarios in her head of meeting him at Wembley, accidentally on purpose. They were all stilted and completely ridiculous and none of them likely to work when he was going back to Atlanta immediately afterwards anyway.

The rain grew heavier, and she pulled her hoodie tighter round her neck as she thought of how awful it would be if she met him and he ignored her completely. She could even see, in her mind's eye, the dreaded Jennifer Crane gloating at her and writing another horrible article for the newspapers. Her breath choked up in her throat and she ran for home. It was only when she was past half way that she remembered that she had forgotten to pick up her pay packet.

She couldn't leave Daniel a message that night. She just couldn't think of anything to say.

Chapter Ten
Rome, October 2009

"Are you sure about this Carrie? This is scarier than I thought it would be. It's not at all like driving at home." Jessica braced her hands on the dashboard as Carrie negotiated the tiny car through the furious stream of traffic encircling the Colosseum.

"It's brilliant! You just have to hoot a lot. That's what all Italians do. We'll be fine!" Carrie yelled as she pushed her hand to the middle of the steering wheel and grinned at the satisfying parp that made other drivers stare at them.

Jessica covered her eyes as a lorry carrying wildly swaying wooden boxes filled with vegetables, came uncomfortably close to their left-hand side. Carrie shook her fist at the driver, but he just blew the girls kisses and blasted forwards in a cloud of hot dust.

"They're all raving mad!" Jessica shrieked. "Next time you hire a car, make sure it comes with a roof at the very least. If we get to the show tonight in one piece it'll be a miracle." Jessica choked on the fumes belching out of the back of the disappearing lorry and then braved another glance at the road before she covered her eyes again.

Carrie laughed at her friend.

"Where's your sense of adventure Jess. This is our last day here and we haven't seen a single bit of the city. All we've seen is Milana wriggling her generous backside about for the last six months. I wanted to see a bit of culture." She flung her arm towards the huge Roman ruins they were passing at that very moment. "I mean, how can we have been in Rome for five days and not seen the Colosseum yet?" She let her eyes wander over the ancient structure. "Even you have to admit that this is a much better view than Milana's bum, and the driving! Whoa! This is great fun. Can't think why I haven't done it before. I passed my test way back in March, but I haven't driven much since."

Jessica let out a small shriek as another car swerved to within inches of them.

"Now you tell me. I thought you passed when you were seventeen. You said you took driving lessons then."

Carrie nodded as she overtook a bus full of school children. The youngsters all waved out of the windows at them and Carrie waved wildly back as they sped past.

"I did, but I failed miserably the first time round. I took a crash course of lessons while the rest of my old crew were doing the cheer team gig for the American footballers. Don't you remember? We had just started rehearsals for this tour. I bought a car soon afterwards, but didn't get much practice what with all the rehearsals for this gig. It's still parked in my parent's driveway. I'm really enjoying the driving now though.

I'm so glad I persuaded the hire company to make special arrangements as I'm under twenty one."

"Oh goody! I am so glad too." Jessica was deeply sarcastic. "Remind me to catch a bus next time you want to see the sights or go shopping."

Carrie pulled a face as she swept her hair out of her eyes.

"Oh come on Jess! We haven't had any fun at all this tour. I haven't even had time to celebrate passing all my 'A' levels and I've not spent a penny of my money on anything for me. It all goes on travelling costs and eating out. I've really scrimped for this little outing. Don't put a damper on the only afternoon we have free for another week." Carrie suddenly swerved into a parking space and came to a grinding halt.

Jess leapt out of the car, clearly relieved that they had stopped at last.

"We had better get shopping quickly then. We have to be back by six at the latest. I don't want Milana going off at us like she did at Dave and Lance. Dave was nearly in tears."

Carrie laughed, locked the car and headed for the nearest shoe shop.

"He's such a sweetie, but so sensitive. Dancing for Milana is fantastic, but she should learn to keep her mouth shut sometimes. It doesn't help having the whole of her dance team upset just because of bad traffic. It wasn't like they were late for her set...Wow!

Those look heels!" She pointed at some frighteningly high heeled, bright red shoes. "They'd be perfect for the after show party!"

Jess peered at the tiny label beneath them and gasped.

"Four hundred and twenty Euros! We'll have them in all three colours shall we?" Sarcasm dripped from Jess's tongue. "And then we'll break our ankles trying to walk in them. Come on Carrie, even if it is our last night in Rome, you'd have to be mad to spend more than a week's wages on them, let's get off the main drag and into the real world."

Carrie looked back wistfully at the beautiful shoes as Jess pulled her into a side street. They wandered in and out of trendy boutiques and past wonderful looking chocolate shops. Carrie bought a tiny, but exquisite evening bag and Jess treated herself to a fine lace blouse. They stopped at a small coffee shop and drank fluffy chocolate and marshmallow topped cappuccinos, then strolled by an alternative route back towards the car. They walked down a narrow street full of electrical retailers and camera shops.

Carrie wasn't looking in any of the windows by now, but just as they were about to cross an intersecting side street she caught sight of the opposite television shop. Her mouth fell open in shock.

Daniel Lewis was on every screen. He laughed

as a female interviewer asked him a question. Then he shook his head and opened his hands expressively as if to prove a point.

Ignoring a hooting car Carrie lunged across the street and into the shop. She ran to the nearest screen and stared at Daniel.

He was definitely wider than when she had last seen him, possibly even taller too going by how tiny the interviewer looked. His face was tanned but his blue eyes seemed a little dull. His lips curved gently as he spoke and she could see the shadow of dark stubble on his upper lip and chin, but Carrie couldn't hear his words as the sound was turned right down.

"Can you turn up the sound please." She turned and asked the salesman. He immediately came over and adjusted the sound by touching the screen.

"Ah, English no? You have a place here that you want to furnish? I can show you the latest models in the audio department too. If you like the sound we can offer…"

Carrie held her finger up as she tried to listen to Daniel. He was smiling good naturedly at the interviewer again. And then she heard his familiar deep voice for the first time in over two years.

"No Lorraine, I'm sorry but I told you I won't answer any questions about my private life. It's far too dull for anyone to be interested in it. Please don't ask me anymore on the subject." He waved his hands dismissively at her.

The camera panned to the woman. She ran the tip of her tongue across her glossy lips and brushed her cheek with her fingertips. Carrie almost laughed at her flirting. The woman adjusted the hem of her skirt pretending to remove invisible fluff. Then she blinked very slowly and deliberately, her eyelashes quivering.

"Okay Daniel, if you insist. Can I ask if you are over the injury that kept you away from the U.K. earlier this year? I hear that a lot of your fans in England were very disappointed that you didn't make it over." Her American drawl dripped from her pouty lips. It looked as if she was almost drooling. Carrie rolled her eyes and hoped someone in the studio had a tissue handy for when her saliva hit the floor.

Carrie took a breath as Daniel nodded, his dark hair flopping slightly over his forehead. She hadn't known that he was injured. Lisa had said nothing about it to her. She frowned as she listened again.

Daniel pushed the hair back from his forehead.

"I'm fine. Thank you for asking. I was terribly disappointed about missing the tour of course. I was looking forward to going home for a spell, but even I couldn't magic away a torn hamstring. I was out of the team for several weeks due to it and the only blessing was that I could catch up on my uni. work. My team mate Paul managed to make it back though so the fans were probably happy enough. The hamstring is fully healed now and this season is going well, so I don't expect to have any more problems." His voice was as soft as Carrie remembered and her heart began to thump wildly.

The interviewer leaned forwards and looked as though she was about to run her fingertips along Daniel's thigh just to make sure it really was recovered, but then she lifted her hand and ran her fingers through her hair instead. Carrie frowned this time. *Couldn't they stop her being quite so obvious?* The woman looked as though she was about to launch herself at Daniel.

Carrie blew out a frustrated breath as the woman tucked her hair behind her ear and rolled her pen between her fingers.

"And when you finish your course here, what will you do then? It's only another six months away. Will we be able to tempt you to stay over here? It's been said that you've made over thirty million dollars in the last two years, what with advertising contracts and sports endorsements." She looked at him for confirmation, but he didn't move a muscle. "Maybe another thirty million dollar contract will do it? I hear that's the amount being discussed." She was leaning forwards again, moving her knees slightly nearer to Daniel's. He shifted uncomfortably in his seat and Carrie noticed that their knees were once again at a respectable distance from each other. Daniel's eyes suddenly became cold, his voice a little distant.

"I only applied for a student visa. I didn't come over here expecting to make a fortune. It just happened that way, so whatever the offer on the table, I'll still have to go back home at the end of my course. I am putting managers in the two sports injury clinics so that they will be able to carry on without me here all the time, though of course I would love to come back on occasions." There was a tiny wrinkle in his brow.

Lorraine came back with a follow up question as she shifted forwards yet again, her knee nearly brushing his.

"So we won't be losing you entirely then. And are you pleased with the way that your thesis has been published early? It's unusual that it's been passed so quickly and that you have been allowed to act upon its recommendations. I understand that the clinics have full waiting lists."

Daniel slanted himself sideways and sat as far back in his chair as possible.

"I'm happy enough with them, but I was hoping to set them up as a preventative exercise class rather than treatment centres. If we can stop the damage occurring through the correct exercise in the first place, then these terrible injuries might never happen. I'm hoping to set up a chain of classes back home in the U.K. so I'll be a little preoccupied for a while after I get back, and then I will have to apply for a visa all over again."

The woman positively fluttered her lashes at him now.

"But I'm sure, what with all the business you are bringing to the city of Atlanta, that if you wanted it, you could be granted an extension to your current visa. Can we tell the viewers that you are going to apply for U. S. citizenship? After all, you will have been here for nearly three years, it's about time you called Atlanta your home." She sounded as though she was going to get down on her knees and beg him to stay. Carrie held her breath, waiting for Daniel's reply. He smiled widely at the woman.

"It's a bit early for a decision of that importance, but you can tell your viewers whatever you like, doesn't mean that I'm going to agree to any of it." He shut his mouth firmly as the interviewer looked taken aback for an instant and then Daniel turned his head away from her. He pressed his huge hands onto the chair's armrests and moved as if to stand up. The camera panned round to the woman only.

"Well there you have it. Another straight answer from the world famous Daniel Lewis."

Her fixed smile wavered for an instant as she glanced to her side, obviously unhappy about the way the interview had ended, and then she shuffled some papers around in front of her. She cleared her throat slightly and then looked back up into the camera and

165

went onto the next item.

Carrie stood back from the screen. The assistant moved forwards again.

"Yes, as you can hear, the sound quality is excellent. It's the same with all the…"

Carrie ignored the assistant, turned quickly and left the shop. She didn't know whether to laugh or cry. She had missed all the football in the spring, just in case she bumped into Daniel when he didn't want to see her and it turned out that he hadn't come over anyway. She couldn't believe Lisa hadn't told her that he was injured. They had called each other nearly every day and she had gone on and on about how much she was missing both Paul and Daniel. It didn't make sense.

And a thirty million dollar contract on top of what he had already earned. Sixty million in all! Carrie's mind boggled at the amount. It was incredible. There was no way he was going to turn it down if offered. Her shoulders slumped and she barely heard Jess waffling on beside her.

"He's absolutely gorgeous isn't he? I adore him and completely understand why you wanted to see him. He's so tall and beyond handsome. Six foot six and completely ripped! I don't think that television had good colour though. His eyes didn't look as blue as they should be, but all that dark, hair. Mmmmm

166

Fabulous! Makes you want to run your fingers right through it. And I could get my hands on his pecks anytime. Phwarrr!" Jessica rolled her eyes as she waffled on, swinging her carrier bag as they walked.

Carrie mused at her side and cut in when Jessica eventually took a breath.

"I think he looks tired. Or maybe you're right and the colour wasn't right on the television. His eyes are definitely brighter, more sapphire in real life. When we were together two years ago they seemed a lot more intense. He looks good though, and I think he may actually have grown even taller. The climate obviously suits him."

Jess had stopped in the middle of the pavement and Carrie looked back at her.

"You were with Daniel Lewis! Carrie Denton! Why didn't you tell me this before? You've been holding out on me. Come on, I want to know all the gory details." She demanded loudly as other shoppers stared at her.

Carrie shrugged and carried on walking down the street as Jess caught up with her.

"There aren't any gory details, more's the pity. I've known him for years, since I was about six. We were neighbours and used to walk to school together, but I only realized that I really liked him when I hit fifteen. Way too late of course! Fool!" She muttered under her breath. "But then on the last day of our

167

exams I dislocated my shoulder and he put it back in for me. He spent the next few days giving me physio so I could get back to full strength and we sort of spent the summer together, in between the dancing. He even came and saw me dance at a couple of gigs. For a while I thought there might be the chance of something between us, but whenever I thought he was going to kiss me or tell me how he felt, he always backed off. I still don't know why because I was way too shy to ask him, but it was obvious that he liked me as a friend." She sighed deeply and then shrugged again. "Anyway, if it wasn't for him and his fantastic physio, I wouldn't be dancing now."

Jess was staring, open mouthed with envy.

"God Carrie! You lucky cow. He can do physio on me any time he likes. Will you be seeing him again when he gets back home?"

Carrie shrugged and shook her head.

"I have no idea Jess. A thirty million dollar contract is one hell of an incentive to keep him in Atlanta. He must be torn if that's what they are offering and that's on top of what he already earns. I'm not stupid enough to think that I have anywhere near that kind of pulling power."

They rounded the corner and spotted their car fifty meters away. There was a tow truck parked in front of it and two men in overalls were just about to attach chains around the wheels. Carrie spoke to Jess

168

rapidly.

"I know you are a fantastic dancer, but do you think you can do a little acting too? Shove that bag up your shirt and slow down. I'll tell them that I'm taking you to hospital."

She didn't wait for an answer, but ran ahead and began imploring the two men in very broken Italian. She waved her hand towards her friend who was walking along the pavement with a very convincing waddle, her front now bulging forward. Jess put her hands in the small of her back and winced painfully. The two men hesitated for a moment and pointed to a sign further along the road. They started back on the chains. Carrie looked up at the sign. It was a disabled parking area and Carrie quite obviously had no badge. She frowned and then looked at Jess meaningfully. Jess puffed up to the car at last. She opened the door and sat down heavily. She gave a tiny cry of pain and the two tow truck men looked up again quickly. Jess somehow managed to squeeze a couple of tears out of her eyes, probably of laughter Carrie thought, and then she began to rock backwards and forwards as she held her stomach gently.

That was enough for the two men. They rolled their eyes, wrapped up their chains and climbed back into their truck. Carrie hopped in over the top of the car door and Jess pulled hers shut. The truck moved forwards and Carrie steered out of the parking space quickly.

Jess waited until they had passed the truck, throwing her hand up over her eyes and remembering to look slightly faint, just in case the driver was still watching them. When they rounded the next corner she pulled the bags out from under her shirt and bellowed with laughter.

"I can't believe we just got away with that. What a pair of idiots! That just goes to show how stupid men can be, though I must say it felt really nice being pregnant." She caressed her now flat stomach gently. "All homely and lovely, even if it was for only about a minute. Okay, I'm convinced. If the dancing ever falls flat on its face, I'll take up a career in acting." She laughed again.

They high fived and Carrie laughed along with her as she drove as fast as possible back to the concert hall.

Her spirits were high, verging on the euphoric. She had driven abroad for the first time and had a wonderful afternoon shopping. She had seen and heard Daniel, and although he hadn't promised he was coming home, he hadn't said he wasn't either. They had enjoyed a mad adventure with the car. Now, they were going to spend the evening doing what they loved best and, to top it all, get paid for it too. She didn't think life could get any sweeter.

She left her message to Daniel early that night. She knew the after show party would carry on late into the night.

"I saw you on the television in an electrical shop today Dan. I was shopping and I spotted you through the window. Well, I couldn't miss you really as you were up there on every screen. I thought that interviewer was going to eat you. You really should try not to look quite so delicious. I'm in Rome and it's fantastic! Come back with me some day. I love you."

Chapter Eleven
April 2010, Athens

"Hi mum. Happy birthday. How old are...I mean how are you?" Carrie giggled down the phone at her mother's sharp intake of breath.

"Cheek! You should never ask a woman of a certain age how old she is. It's unseemly." Carrie could hear her mum smiling as she spoke.

"Sorry I couldn't ring earlier. We had to do a thing in a children's home. Milana was talking to the kids and we had to dance. It's all just publicity for Milana's shows really, but you should have seen the children's faces when we all walked in. They couldn't believe it."

Helen sounded impressed.

"Oh darling, that sounds wonderful. It's so good that you can fit in some nice things to do. Even if it is a publicity stunt, I'm sure it was much appreciated."

Carrie made a strange sound in her throat.

"Well, it would have been lovely if Milana hadn't called a three hour rehearsal immediately afterwards. Not including her of course. She doesn't need to practice at all...She's a complete tyrant, most of the time. I'll be honest mum, I wish she hadn't been quite so successful. She's sold out everywhere so she's extending the tour by a couple of months."

Helen sighed softly.

"I don't know whether to be pleased or disappointed. We're really missing you. I know you had the break over Christmas, but Jim was being such a bore then. We can't wait to see you back here permanently." Helen sounded almost close to tears.

Carrie spoke softly.

"Even dad?" She regretted saying it as soon as it came out of her mouth. "Oh mum, I'm sorry, it's just that he asks if I have a boyfriend or who I'm going out with all the time. As if most of the guys in the group aren't gay anyway. I don't get chance to meet anyone outside of the team and he knows I just want to be sure with Daniel." She rushed her explanation and heard Helen sigh again. "Are you okay, mum? You sound really down."

Helen sniffed down the line.

"I'm fine. Feeling my age I suppose. Carrie, I just want you home for a while. A year is too long, even if you have rung nearly every other day. Dad really misses you as well you know, whatever he says to your face."

Carrie sighed.

"I know, and I miss you both too, but Athens isn't far, why not come and meet me? We're here for the next week and then we go back over to Spain. You've got the original tour dates. I'm sure there are cheap flights to one of the gigs."

Helen answered quietly.

"Jim doesn't want to leave work. He's worried that if he takes a holiday they'll think he's not up to the work and put him on the redundancy list. He thinks he's too old and crusty to get anything else."

Carrie laughed as she privately agreed with her dad. He was definitely far too crusty.

"He may be crusty, but you need a holiday mum, why don't you come over? I can meet you at the airport. I'm sure Milana won't mind if you come back stage if I can't get you a ticket. It would be fun." She tried to persuade her mother.

Carrie hated to admit it, but she was very homesick. They had spent the best part of the last year either on the road, or in the air. She had loved every minute of the dancing, but it was more tiring than she had ever imagined possible and, not for the first time in her career, she was wondering if there wasn't more to life than dancing behind some "prima donna."

In her last few phone calls to Daniel's mobile she had barely been able to speak, she was so exhausted and on one night her message had been more yawn than actual words.

Milana's behavior was a little better now. At the beginning of the tour she had been almost impossible to work with, throwing her weight about nearly every day and several of the original dancers had soon walked out, but after a few months she had calmed down slightly. As long as she could have her cigarettes any time she wanted them she remained fairly calm. It was only on the odd occasion when the theatre or stage had very sensitive smoke alarms that she sprung a wild and totally irrational hissy fit on them.

Carrie came back to her senses when her mother suddenly said.

"Okay. I'll do it. I'll see what flights are available. Oh, and I forgot to tell you, you had a letter reconfirming your university place. I assumed it was okay and sent off the acceptance forms. I'll give you a call in an hour when I've had time to see when the flights run."

"Yay!" Carrie cried out. "Thanks mum, that's brilliant news. I can't wait to see you. Just don't get a flight that lands after five or you'll be needing a taxi. Speak to you in an hour." She put the phone down and sat smiling to herself.

There was a sudden voice in her ear.

"And what are you so happy about? We're all feeling worn out and miserable and here you are, full of the joys of spring. It's sickening." The team's leading male dancer, Oliver, had walked away from an exhausted group. He was staring down at her.

Carrie grinned at him.

"My mum just confirmed my university place for September and she might be coming to see me. It'll be the first time she's seen me dance with Milana. All my other work was with a boy band. We went on tour, but it was all small stuff, nobody like Milana. I mean, she's huge!"

Oliver slumped down beside her, obviously unimpressed.

"Yeah, huge. You mean her ego or her arse?" He grinned at Carrie as she stuffed her hand in her mouth to hold back her laugh and then he was serious again. "I seem to have been looking at the main attractions huge backside, wriggling about in front of me, for over ten years, or is it twelve? Actually, when I think about it, it could be fifteen. Anyway, it's been so long I've forgotten and my mum has never bothered to come to see me. You're really lucky." He closed his eyes and rubbed his temples.

Carrie gasped in shock.

"Fifteen years! Wow! I don't know how you've done it. I don't think I want to be doing this for the next fifteen years. I can't imagine doing it for another two."

Oliver gave a dry laugh.

"I didn't expect to be doing this for so long myself, but you get sucked into the lifestyle. The years have gone by so fast, but I'm going to have to finish soon, my joints have had it, and I have no idea of what to do next. I've not trained for anything else."

Carrie nudged him.

"Oh cheer up Oliver. You're not finished yet. You've got years left in you. You don't look a day over…well over…er." She didn't finish as she looked at his tired face and realized that she couldn't even guess how old he was.

"Thanks." He said flatly and pursed his lips. "That makes me feel a whole lot better. How old do you think I am Carrie? Go on, have a guess. I can take it on the chin." He angled his face slightly away from the light and lifted his chin so that the skin was very taught beneath.

She tried to be kind.

"Thirty-eight? Sorry, sorry." She covered her eyes with her hand at his sudden intake of breath and offended look. "I'm not very good with ages. My mum had me when she was sixteen, and she still looks really young but my dad was completely bald by the time he was thirty, so I can't judge very well. It's probably because you look tired, but then I expect I look like I'm twenty five at the moment and I'm only eighteen." She cringed back in embarrassment.

Oliver sighed deeply.

"Actually you weren't too far out. Only eight years! I'm just over thirty. All the late nights, the horrible make-up, lack of sleep, not to mention the punishment on your body, takes its toll eventually. I started this caper when I was fifteen and became so wrapped up in all the glamour and travelling that I never attempted to do anything else. You have 'A' levels Carrie, I'm glad you're going to use them wisely. University is definitely the right choice. You don't want to end up like me. Thirty plus and nothing to show for it. I really thought this gig was going to make me enough money to get out. Fifty grand sounds a lot but I haven't been able to save a penny. Travelling and the hotels don't come cheap any more. God! I am so fed up with this tour. It's the longest I've ever been on and, quite honestly, I've had enough." He looked up and then made to stand up.

Carrie wished she could think of something to say that would cheer him up. She watched him as he rubbed his knees.

"They troubling you Oliver?" She grimaced for him as he nodded and winced, then she noticed that he was holding his whole body stiffly. "You should do some of my friend Dan's exercises. I don't know the specific ones for knees but the feeling you get from the breathing is fantastic. I once helped a lady give birth using them. She had a ten pound baby completely naturally, didn't even tear. Come on, give them a go." She encouraged as Oliver looked back at her sceptically.

"I'd probably be more impressed if I knew what a ten pound baby looks like. Okay, okay, I'm doing it." He muttered as she glared at him, and moved onto the floor next to Carrie.

Oliver watched her cautiously for a few moments and then sighed as she breathed in and raised her arms above her head. She spread them open and then pushed them as far behind her back as she could reach, gradually stretching them round to her front again. She leaned forwards from the hips and relaxed her body towards the floor. She let out her breath and pushed her arms forward even further, as she remembered the way Daniel had shown her.

Oliver was copying her every move.

"This is so good. Better than our normal cool down. Who did you say you learned this from?"

Carrie noticed that one or two of the other dancers, who had listened to their conversation, had joined them. She concentrated on leaning sideways and took another deep breath, releasing it slowly before she spoke.

"Daniel Lewis. He plays American football and he's doing his thesis on this type of training at the Atlanta University. He used to live near me. Take another breath." Carrie breathed in gently and then breathed in again, filling the whole of her lung space. It was a technique Daniel had used to get as much oxygen around the body as possible.

Oliver almost whispered as he held his breath for a moment.

"I think I know who you mean. Great big fella? I've seen him on the mineral water ads. Well, tell him he should ditch the water adverts, he needs to bottle this. It's a dancer's dream, like a deep massage from within, one that you can do yourself anytime. It's fantastic." His breath came out in a long whoosh.

The whole dance team now sat on the floor. There was a collective deep breath and a swaying of bodies. One or two of the dancers moaned as they relaxed. There were groans of relief all around the floor. The sound of complete relaxation ran around the hall as everyone felt the tension fall from their limbs.

Carrie glanced over to the bench where she and Oliver had sat earlier. Her phone was buzzing quietly. She breathed deeply once more and then reached out for it. She almost giggled as everyone else in the room reached out with one arm too.

She flipped the phone into her palm, hoping that nobody had noticed it, and glanced at the screen. It was a text from her mother. She carefully touched the screen so that she could read it.

"Carrie, sorry love. Flights all full for the next three weeks. I forgot it's the Easter holidays. Too upset to talk. Will ring again in the morning."

"Oh no!" Carrie couldn't help herself. Oliver looked up.

"Problem?" He whispered out of the corner of his mouth.

Carrie rolled her eyes at him and lifted her arms above her head again.

"Mum can't get any flights. It's the Easter holidays." She tried not to let her disappointment show as she breathed out and let her arms drop gently to her sides. She shook them lightly and the whole room gave a gentle sigh. General chatting broke out with one or two of the dancers coming over to ask questions. It was obvious that they all felt more relaxed.

The dancers suddenly fell silent. Milana stepped out of her dressing room, cigarette hanging from the corner of her glossy lips as she walked over to where Carrie was now standing with Oliver. She stepped right between them, forcing Oliver out of her way.

She didn't offer any preamble but took the cigarette from her mouth and blew smoke directly in Carrie's face.

"What was that you were doing with the dancers? It was very effective, like a flowing river of people, perfect for my second number. I want to see it in tonight's show." She stared at Carrie waiting for some kind of response.

Carrie coughed slightly and wafted the smoke away.

"I can't do that Milana. It's not my technique. A friend of mine was helping me over an injury and we used it extensively then, but it's his therapy not mine. I can't steal the idea from him and put it in a show." She went to turn away when Milana caught hold of her shoulder. Her freshly manicured fingernails dug painfully into Carrie's skin leaving her gasping in surprise.

Milana hissed menacingly.

"I said I want it in tonight's show." She raised her voice to the dancers. "Come on everyone, Miss. Carol Dentrom is going to show us all how to put this to my music." Milana was beckoning the dancers to come nearer.

Carrie pulled herself away from Milana's nails and pressed her lips together. *After a whole year Milana still hadn't even bothered to remember her name!* It shook her as she realized how unimportant to the star she really was. She spoke stiffly.

"It's Carrie Denton, Milana and I'm not telling or showing you anything. It's an exercise regime, not a dance. My friend would be furious with me if I showed you before he's had time to make his final presentation on it." Carrie was adamant. She stepped back as Milana took another long drag from her cigarette and appeared to suddenly swell, overshadowing Carrie's compact form.

He words came out like splintering ice particles.

"Show me now Ms. Denton. Don't try and play games with me. It won't work. I'm the star here. I can have exactly what I want in my show and I want that workout, so stop messing about and start showing the dancers." She dropped the end of her cigarette onto the floor just in front of Carrie's foot and ground it out with her heel.

Carrie faced her. She could hear Oliver breathing furiously down her neck. He placed his hand on the indentations left by Milana's overlong fingernails and squeezed Carrie gently, offering his support silently. She could see Jessica's exhausted face, pale and drawn behind Milana. She saw Jessica narrow her eyes and shake her head just once.

Carrie didn't need to be told by Oliver or Jess not to tell Milana a thing. There was no way that she would ever betray Daniel. She lifted her chin defiantly.

"I'm sorry Milana, but I can't. I can choreograph a dance routine if you want, but it won't involve those moves." She squared her slender shoulders at the statuesque diva.

Milana's face began to discolour. It changed from a flushed pink to a darker red and then to purple, before her lips turned blue with rage. The skin at the underside of her jaw began to shake. Carrie wondered for a moment if she was having some kind of seizure but she eventually opened her mouth and spat out.

"Why you little…Don't you know who I am? I'll see that you never work in this industry again. You cannot speak to me like that." The loose skin under Milana's jaw wobbled like an unset jelly.

Carrie almost laughed at her.

"Milana, I won't teach what isn't mine to show. It would be totally unprofessional. You wouldn't sing any of Kylie Minogue's songs without her permission, so don't expect me to put anything of Daniel Lewis's in your show."

Milana's eyes suddenly grew wide. And then her expression changed completely. She laughed delightedly flipping her hair as she pulled a new cigarette from the packet she dug from her pocket. She lit it quickly.

"Oh, they're Danny's moves." She drawled. "well why didn't you say so in the first place? I know Danny personally. I have done for years. He won't mind you telling me. I'll fix it all up with him when I see him in September. I'm taking my tour to the States and if you want to be part of it, you had better start showing the dancers right now." She blew smoke over Carrie again.

Carrie fixed her with a disbelieving look.

"Danny!" She exploded with laughter and shook her head as she wafted the vile smelling fumes out of her face. "I've heard him called a few things but Danny is certainly not one of them. You are such a liar Milana. There's no way that you know Daniel. Apart from the fact that he's about half your age and went to school with me, he detests people who smoke. He wouldn't give someone as self-serving and small minded as you, the time of day."

Oliver suddenly guffawed loudly behind her and Milana's face fell as she realized that her bluff had been called. Oliver rammed his hand over his mouth and tried to stop himself but couldn't. He bellowed with infectious laughter and the other dancers began to join in.

Milana stared in complete outrage as sniggers erupted from all around the floor.

"None of you will ever work for me again! You are all fired! As of right now. Get out the lot of you!" She fumed and swirled away in a haze of smoke, towards her dressing room.

The other dancers quietened down fairly rapidly and Jess spoke to the room in general.

"Do you think she meant that? Do you think we're really all fired?" Her voice was half way between scared and delighted.

Oliver pulled in a deep breath and controlled himself at last. He spoke to the dancers as they all looked to him for advice.

"I don't care whether she meant it or not. We were paid yesterday so there's nothing holding us here. I'm getting out before she changes her mind and makes me do these last ten shows. I'm completely done in so I'm going to take this fabulous opportunity and travel to pastures new. I've just about enough money for the bus fare from here to London. Maybe I'll start teaching in Covent Garden. Whatever I do has to be better than putting up with this old cow. I know the bus will take a couple of days, but it's not as though we're not used to travelling and at least it's cheap. Anyone coming with me?"

There was a moment's stillness and then a collective breath as the whole company dashed for their dressing rooms. There were several shouts of,

"Book a seat for me Oliver." And then they started leaving in droves.

Carrie picked up her bag and caught up with Jessica as she was making for the door.

"Hey! You going without me?" Carrie linked her arm through her friend's.

Jess smiled a little hesitantly.

"I hope we're all doing the right thing here Carrie. We could end up being very sorry about all of this."

Carrie shrugged.

"No, I don't think so. There are loads of bigger fish than Milana in the sea. I somehow don't think we're going to be sorry at all. I'm going to collect my stuff from the hostel and then I'm taking a sightseeing tour on the way home. I'm not sorry that I've done all the travelling, but all I seem to have seen is the inside of one theatre after another, and they all look exactly the same after a while. I've managed to save a little and I want to see the sights we missed on the way here and then go home and get ready for university in September. I want to spend a little time relaxing first."

Jess grinned widely.

"When you put it like that, it sounds brilliant. I wonder if there are any opportunities at university for oldies like me."

Carrie spluttered back at her.

"Oldie? At twenty four! Come on Jess, of course there will be something. I think you just have to take the bull by the horns and go for it. Now let's go and clear our digs before Milana really does change her mind and keep us here as her prisoners."

Carrie couldn't help the laughter in her tone as she left her message to Daniel while on the bus later that night.

"Hey! I hear you have friends in high places! I just gave up my day job because of you! I hope you haven't grown a head or arse as big as Milana's! I love you Danny!"

Chapter Twelve
July 3rd 2010

"Carrie! Over here!" Her mum was waving madly from behind the barrier.

They fought through the crowd and hugged as they reached each other at last.

"Sorry I'm late, the train was delayed in Paris for half an hour. Where's dad?" Carrie asked craning her neck as she peered through the crowd for a glimpse of her father. They hadn't left each other on the best of terms, and the atmosphere had been a little frosty at times over the Christmas break, but she was now desperate to see him.

"He's bringing the car round to the front of the station. I asked him so we didn't have to walk miles with your suitcase, and I wanted to have a quick private talk with you too." Helen glanced up as the moved along the concourse.

"What's the matter mum? Is there some kind of problem? Don't tell me they have turned down my university place after all." Carrie started to panic. Now that she had made the decision, she was looking forward to going.

Helen flapped her hands.

"No, silly, nothing like that. I just wanted to warn you so you didn't get a shock if you see the adverts. Daniel is coming home."

Carrie gasped and stopped dead in the corridor. A man bumped into her back and mumbled an apology as he stumbled past. She picked up the pace again.

"When? Come on mum, when?" She was desperate to know.

Helen pulled her over to the wall where they could speak without being trampled on.

"It was on the television. He's giving his first interview just after he gets off the plane tomorrow. Apparently he's travelling straight to the studio from the airport. It's been advertised for days on the local news because that scheming ex-friend of yours is doing the interview. You remember, the one that was bullying you. She's had a right makeover and made a bit of a name for herself. Calls herself Jenna now, but I'd know her anywhere after that article she wrote about you last year. Lying bitch!"

Carrie could barely breathe. She ignored her mum's indignation. She couldn't care less about Jennifer Crane. She needed to hear more about Daniel.

"Is he coming home really? I mean, did he say anything about coming home here?" Her mind was whirling with the information.

"Jenna didn't say, but Lisa and Paul are definitely coming to see you. They're bringing little Tommy. Won't that be lovely! I can't wait to see our God son for real. I know that you both keep in touch normally, but since you've been sightseeing Lisa has been calling here. She rang last night to confirm that it was okay to drop in. They're coming over straight after the interview, so I suspect Daniel's coming too." Helen was smiling widely.

Carrie suddenly bent forwards feeling slightly faint. She put her head between her knees and took some deep breaths, desperate to calm her pounding heart. It had been nearly three years since she had seen Daniel Lewis and she had thought that by now she would be able to control her feelings. It was obvious that she couldn't. She was suddenly more than relieved that she hadn't agreed to a quick trip into Belgium with Jess before coming home. She might have missed him. She looked up at her mother and then gasped as she realized how little time she had to prepare.

"Tomorrow! Oh God mum. I've spent the last few weeks sleeping practically rough while Jess and I were touring. We were on a tight budget and those hostels are very basic you know. I look a right state. Just look at my hair, and my nails!" She threw up her hands in despair. "Why is he coming so soon? Surely the football season hasn't finished yet? I didn't think I'd see him until September."

Helen brushed her hand over her daughters flushed cheek.

"Calm down a minute. The football season may not have finished, but his visa has run out. He only went to the States as a student and the college term finished at the end of June. He has to come back here and reapply if he wants to stay longer. But don't worry about how you look. I guessed that you'd be doing this sightseeing on less than nothing. I've booked us a session at the spa for this afternoon. Can't have my daughter looking like something the cat's dragged in, just as her boyfriend gets home. I wouldn't like him to think that you hadn't bothered. And I fancied a bit of a pamper myself. It'll be a lovely way to spend the afternoon catching up together. I want to hear everything about all the countries you have been to."

Carrie stood up straight again. She could feel the pulse in her throat throbbing deeply.

"Thanks mum. I don't know what I'd do without you."

Helen tucked her arm through her daughter's.

"No, I'm sure you wouldn't, but please don't mention the spa bit to your father. He's still prejudiced against Daniel, though not for the same reasons as before. I think now it's more that he couldn't prove that he was either a womaniser or gay. The most he's come up with so far is that Daniel might be a bit boring because he likes to go fishing on the odd occasion." Helen gave a small laugh. "I think he's really disappointed that he can't say, "I told you so." And I don't suppose he'd like it if he thought we were going to any special effort for Daniel."

Carrie started walking again. She could see her

father standing outside the car waving at her. She quickened her step and soon he was hugging her madly.

"I've missed you so much. Carrie, I'm so sorry we fell out about that Daniel kid. Do you think we can forget how stupid I was." He sounded slightly choked.

Carrie nodded into his shoulder.

"Of course dad, but you have to remember that he will still be my friend when he comes home, no matter what." Carrie pulled herself out of his grasp and looked up at his face.

Jim shrugged.

"Well, as your mum put it once before. Now you're over eighteen, there's not much I can do about who your friends are anyway, but it wasn't that I didn't like him Carrie. I just didn't want him to mess you around."

Carrie eyed her father sceptically but then decided to give it up. I wasn't worth the argument right now. Right now she wanted to get herself looking her best in the hope that Daniel still wanted something, anything to do with her.

"I know that dad, but you should trust people a little more. Dan would never mess me around. He's not that type of man." She picked up her case and threw it into the boot of the car.

Jim opened the car door for her.

"Huh, trouble is, now that he's been away for so

long, none of us know what kind of man he's grown into. He's doing some kind of interview thing tomorrow. And even if he does stay here after that, I don't suppose he'll have time to be friends with the likes of us anymore. He's a multi-millionaire now Carrie, not only a famous footballer, but into all the modelling and advertising, way above our league."

Carrie rolled her eyes at her mum. This was going to be harder than she had thought. She climbed into the car as her mum spoke again.

"I don't know why you would think that Jim, after all, Lisa and Paul are coming to see Carrie tomorrow to introduce Tommy. I'm so excited! He's only just over two. I bought some toys for him to play with."

Jim snorted indignantly.

"You should have just filled the fridge with food. If Paul is going to be here, he's going to eat us out of house and home. I bet that's one thing that won't have changed about that Daniel, if he bothers to come over at all. I bet he can still eat mountains of food. I'm going to move some of the furniture tonight so we can fit them all in."

Carrie laughed at her father and sat back in the car. She was so glad to be home. The train journey from Paris had been quick, but she still felt exhausted. She wondered how she and her mother were going to keep the trip to the spa a secret. It would be obvious if one moment she looked like a wet dishrag and the next some kind of glamour model. She watched the familiar sights of London pass by and then as they neared Harrow, Jim veered off the usual route.

"Hey, which way are we going? Have they put in a new road while I've been away?" Carrie sat forward in her seat and stared out of the window as they turned towards the M4.

Jim grinned and put his hand on Helen's knee. He gave it a little squeeze.

"No, I'm just taking you straight to the spa. Can't have either of you talking to a millionaire while looking like a dog's dinner. Wouldn't like you to let the side down, even if it doesn't mean anything."

Carrie slumped back in her seat again and giggled as her mum pulled in a breath.

Jim carried on.

"Well, you can't keep a secret like that Helen. The spa phoned you yesterday evening to confirm your appointment. They are obviously very keen on getting you both there. They rang three times. Because you hadn't bothered telling me about it, the first couple of times I didn't understand a word of what they going on about. There was something wrong with the line. It was all distorted and echoing, but I thought they said 'Thirteen thirty, at five.' Then some kind of reference number and a hope that you wouldn't be delayed. Sounded like something out of 'Mission Impossible.' It was just as well some other young woman rang again about five minutes later and explained properly. 'One thirty until five o'clock' and you've been booked in for three or four treatments depending on how soon you get there. They hoped you weren't going to be late."

He pulled the car off the motorway and a few minutes later they turned into a private drive. A huge house stood at the end of the avenue of trees that lined the driveway and several ladies in short white jackets came out to greet them. Carrie and Helen climbed out of the car and Jim waved merrily.

"See you at five when you're both even more beautiful than you are already." And he drove away leaving both Carrie and Helen speechless.

Carrie wondered if she should leave Daniel a message that night. She didn't know if there was any point. In the end, after several moments' hesitation she spoke firmly into the phone, leaving what she hoped would be her last message to him.

Chapter Thirteen
July 4th Heathrow Airport

"Are you sure you gave her the right flight number?" Daniel was looking over the top of his bodyguard's head, scanning the waiting crowd.

Paul slapped his friend on his shoulder with one hand and tucked Tommy closer into his side with the other. Tommy turned his chubby face into his father's shoulder, away from the flashing cameras.

"Course I did. I spoke to her father and I rang twice to check he'd got it. And we're right on time. Don't worry, she'll be here." Paul spoke as confidently as possible. He had wondered if Mr. Denton had written the message down at the time and now he was a little worried himself. "Mind you, I wasn't expecting this amount of people to turn up. *It's a regular 4th of July.*" He added in a horrible impersonation of an American accent.

Lisa clutched at Paul's arm.

"What a crush! I hope there's a car waiting for us. I don't think I could stand to be left in a taxi queue."

Paul nodded as Daniel scanned the crowd again.

"I would have hired us a car but the television company said they are sending a limo. I think that woman is going to be with it, just to make sure we don't run off before you give your interview Dan."

196

Paul gave a chuckle.

Daniel scowled over at his friend.

"Can't imagine why I agreed to an interview now. What an idiot. And it's not like we can't afford a car of our own. We could have hired one each." And then there was a small break in the crowd and a short, heavily made up young woman hustled through.

She stuck out her hand and a microphone at the same time. Daniel looked down at her and shook her hand briefly, pulling his fingers away from hers when she didn't let go immediately.

"Hi Daniel. I hope you remember me." She breathed up at him in a sickly voice. She didn't wait for a response, but carried on immediately. "Jenna Crane. West London Television. We were at school together. Harrow High?" She looked up at Daniel hopefully. Daniel stared back down at her and frowned as though trying to remember.

"No, I don't remember you." He said quite bluntly and looked away from her, his eyes scanning the crowd once again.

Paul looked at his friend in surprise. He knew Daniel was on edge but it was unlike him to be rude to anyone.

Jenna Crane obviously didn't notice, she didn't bat an eyelid and carried on smiling widely.

"No matter, it was a big school and a long time ago. I don't suppose you remember many people from there anyway. Well, except for this gentleman of course, but then you do seem to spend every waking moment together so it would be hard not to remember him." She edged her way between Paul and Daniel as Daniel stared down at her in utter amazement. "I have a car waiting outside, if you'd like to come with me." She gave a hurried glance at Lisa. "I'm sorry, I didn't think about a booster seat for your kid. Shall I call you a cab with one? I can take Daniel onto the studio and you can do…well, you can do just what you feel like." Jenna turned from Lisa dismissively.

Paul stepped away from Jenna and passed Tommy to Lisa. He spoke to her in a low voice close to her ear.

"Look, I don't know what her game is, but you don't have to be a part of it. I'll call you and Tommy a cab. Can you go round to Carrie's house? See if her dad knows what's going on. I'd better go with Dan, he's obviously upset she's not here. There's probably a simple explanation. I bet airport security have kept the public out or something like that. We'll meet you at Carrie's later."

Lisa nodded and Paul kissed her briefly to a mad clicking of cameras.

Jenna gushed wildly.

"Ooh young love! Perhaps we can get some back ground on you too Paul, though obviously you are not quite as famous as Daniel."

Paul shook his head and laughed.

"Not a chance Jenna. I may not be as famous, but then I'm probably not as polite as Dan either. You'd better stick with him. I'll just tag along for the ride."

They had reached the picking up point and a long limousine swept into view. Paul made everyone wait until he was sure Lisa was put into a cab with Tommy and all their luggage, then he climbed into the limousine with Jenna, Daniel and what felt like a whole film crew.

Jenna talked Daniel through the coming live interview the whole way to the studios. A couple of times he nodded at something Jenna said, but most of the journey he just stared morosely out of the window.

Paul knew that something was terribly wrong. Daniel was normally fairly chatty, conversation coming easily to his lips, but now his face was sombre, his forehead wrinkled into a frown and his eyes dull. He barely spoke a word and his fingertips continually drummed on his knee.

Paul talked incessantly to cover for Daniel's silence. He was desperate to speak to his friend, to reassure him, but he couldn't say a word in front of Jenna. It would be all over the news in seconds.

Daniel sat coiled in the leather seat. His expression grim and Paul could see that he was about to go off like an erupting volcano. But there was nothing he could say to ease Daniel's tension. All he

199

could do was stay close to his friend's side and be there to catch the fallout when the explosion eventually took place.

Another television crew met them at the studio and Daniel was rushed through to make-up. Then twenty minutes later Jenna came into the dressing room and asked him to come through to the studio.

Paul watched from the sidelines as the camera crew fell silent and Jenna introduced the Atlanta Raiders youngest ever Captain and highest ever goal scorer. Then the interview began.

Jenna started by asking about the transition from English rugby to American football and Daniel explained the first few weeks training that he and Paul had undergone. He answered her questions on his studies and the college in general. He was a little more reticent when she asked about his thirty million dollar contract and whether it was going to be renewed and then she asked about his living arrangements.

Daniel shook his head.

"Sorry Jenna. I don't discuss my personal life." He began to tap his foot slightly.

Jenna spread her hands in mock shock.

"But Daniel, the public are fascinated by you. Successful beyond anyone's wildest dreams at the age of twenty one, and no one knows about your home life. You must be able to give us something to get out teeth into. Your relationship with Paul and his...err, his wife, for instance. I understand that you all live together. A real ménage a trois." Jenna's voice gave the slightest lift and even Paul's eyes boggled at her insinuation. He saw Daniel sit a little straighter in his chair, his fingers drumming on the arm rest.

"I'm not answering any questions about my private life Jenna." His voice was very low, his eyebrows furrowed and his sapphire eyes became midnight dark.

Jenna sat forward as if about to pounce on him.

"Oh, come on Daniel, you can tell us. We all know that you've lived with Paul Edmonds since you left England for the States. I can't think why you need to keep it a secret."

Daniel positively glowered at her now.

"It's no secret. I'm just not answering any questions on it. Now please ask something else or we will have to conclude this interview."

Jenna looked as though she were about to ask again, but then she backed off as she caught his furious expression.

"Okay, if you insist. Now about your thesis on sports injuries and the completely new technique of keeping fit while injured. As you seem to do so much together, can you confirm to the viewers if Paul is involved with you in that? As a 'hands on' sort of friend?"

Daniel put his hands firmly on the arms of the

201

chair and started to push himself up. Jenna reached out and made to push him down again, but Daniel whisked his arm from under hand before she could touch him.

"Oh dear, Daniel." She laughed again. "We do seem to have hit a bit of a raw nerve. I only want to discover your true personality, not the image that you live behind. Well, I can't really see why your private relationship with Paul bothers you anyway, everyone has one or two guilty secrets. If you are in the public eye, you must expect them to be exposed."

Daniel turned on her, his face like stone. He leaned forwards slightly in his chair, his expression dangerous.

"Yes. I expect we all have a secret or two. Like you for instance. Actually I lied to you at the airport earlier, I do remember you." He waited while Jenna gave a delighted smile and then carried on. "I did a little checking before we came over. I recalled that your name was really Jennifer and that you hide your real name just in case people remember what a vile woman you really are." He looked fiercely into her eyes. She was momentarily stunned and then he spoke suspiciously softly again. "So maybe that's just one of your guilty secrets, but I know another one too Jennifer. Perhaps your viewers would like to share it with me. Do you remember, Jennifer?" He emphasized her real name. "Do you remember when you were sixteen, you were so jealous of your best friend gaining a dancing contract, that you tried to sabotage her whole future by slamming her arm in a fire door. You and one or two friends managed to dislocate her shoulder…And, as if trying to end her career wasn't enough for you, you wrote up spiteful articles and then outright lies about her relationship with me." He paused, but Jenna didn't respond. Her whole face was a mask of shock. He hissed at her. "So is that your other guilty secret Jennifer, the fact that you are a nasty, scheming, two faced bitch who just likes to hurt people who do better than you? Perhaps you like it now that your true personality has been exposed to your viewers by an eye witness." He stood up swiftly, shoving his chair backwards into a wall and then moved across the studio. There was stunned silence on the studio floor as he strode towards Paul and said.

"Come on, let's ditch the bodyguards and get out of here. I can drop you off so that you can meet Lisa. I'm going back to Heathrow. With a bit of luck I can get a flight back out to Atlanta this afternoon."

And then the cameras cut back to Jennifer, still sitting in her chair while her mouth opened and closed soundlessly.

Chapter Fourteen
At the same time in Harrow

"What the hell is she talking about!" Lisa was standing in front of the television screen, her fists clenched in fury. "She's insinuating that we have some kind of threesome going! A "ménage a trois!" Did she really say that? What a stinking cow! What the hell is she suggesting?" She was totally shocked.

Carrie sat with her head in her hands. Seeing Daniel rattled like this was appalling.

"Well she hasn't changed much! I don't think it's about a threesome Lisa. I think she's trying to get him to come out of the closet on live television."

Lisa looked at her in total confusion.

"What closet? They're in a studio…" And then it sunk in. "Oh! The gay thing."

Carrie looked kindly at Lisa.

"It's okay, you don't have to cover up for him, I've suspected it for years. And you've told me yourself that he never goes out with any women in America…Do you know what Lisa? I think he's in love with Paul. He probably lives with you two still, just so he can be near him."

Lisa started an almost maniacal laugh, but caught her breath quickly as she saw Carrie shake her head.

"Are you mad Carrie! Daniel isn't gay, you idiot. And especially not with my Paul! My God, Paul would

204

go bonkers! I can't believe you think it still. They're just best friends and the house is enormous, it makes sense that we all live together. I thought I'd explained, Daniel has his own wing to himself. Why would he want to bother living anywhere else?"

Carrie looked up at the screen again just as the odious Jennifer tried to shoot yet another barb. He fought back, his revealing words rocking Carrie to the core, and then he stalked off the set. She could barely believe it as she heard his voice, angry and tight, coming from somewhere out of camera shot.

"I'm going back to Heathrow. With a bit of luck I can get a flight back out to Atlanta this afternoon."

Carrie sat back and stared at Jenna's gawping, silent face for a few seconds and then the screen cut to adverts. She tried to take in Lisa's words and then she swivelled round to her mother who was bouncing a laughing Tommy on her knee.

"Did you hear that mum? He said he was going back to Heathrow. He's not coming here at all." Her face was a solid mask, her voice completely hollow with shock.

Lisa spun around.

"He can't go back! He's meant to be coming with us. Something has gone dreadfully wrong Carrie. I'm sure he was expecting you to be at the airport today. I know Paul rang your dad with the flight numbers yesterday. And I overheard Daniel talking to

Paul a while back about some sort of pact you two had made. He always said he couldn't speak to you because it would break his word."

Carrie stood up and wrung her hands.

"What pact? I don't know what you're talking about. The last time I saw Daniel was at that hotel in Birmingham after we finished our first tour together, and we never said anything about any pact. He left after he put me to bed. You have to remember the night Lisa. It was the night you got pregnant!" The desperation in her tone was obvious.

Lisa tried very hard not to go mushy with the memory.

"Of course I remember the night Carrie, but Paul and I hardly saw you and Daniel. As you point out we were otherwise engaged." She looked fondly at Tommy.

Carrie was frantic now.

"But how does he expect me to be somewhere when I don't know what he's arranged? I didn't know about the flight. I didn't even know you were coming home until mum told me as I arrived back from Paris yesterday." Carrie caught hold of her friend's arms and shook her imploringly.

Jim suddenly shuffled into the lounge from the kitchen. He had been listening to the conversation. He coughed nervously a couple of times before Helen almost shouted at him.

"For goodness sake Jim, I can tell you've got something to do with this. Spit it out. This is important."

Jim hesitated for a second longer.

"It's just that…you remember me saying that I found out about the spa because someone reconfirmed the booking, well I also said there had been two other messages, neither of which I understood because of the echoing and distortion, but now, hearing what Lisa says, I think now that they may have been flight details."

Tommy slid from Helen's knee as her arms fell limp at her sides. He ran to his mother and clutched at her leg.

Helen shook her head in defeat.

"Oh God Jim, you idiot. What have you gone and done?"

Jim puffed out his chest.

"Now hang on just a moment! There's no need to take that attitude with me. How was I to know it was some kind of message for Carrie? If you ask me he's just trying to get out of coming here. He doesn't want to be associated with the likes of us. He's gone way too upmarket with his thirty million dollars to come anywhere near here."

Lisa picked up Tommy and leapt forwards.

"That's ridiculous Jim. Daniel's not a snob. He loves it around here and wanted to come back. He's

207

bought a house not far away so I know he wants to be here. And apart from that, he and Paul have been selected for the England rugby squad! The contracts have all been signed, and his visa has run out anyway. He can't just go back to America!"

Carrie didn't have time to gasp before there was a loud hammering on the front door. Everyone jumped as Jim went to answer it and he was almost crushed behind the door as Paul thundered through into the lounge.

He faced Carrie, his expression furious. He didn't wait for her to open her mouth before he shouted.

"He's gone! My best friend has gone and it's all your fault! Why couldn't you have been at the airport like he asked? Even if you don't want him, you could have been there. We could have sorted everything else out afterwards, but now…I don't know what's going to happen now." His angry tone was tinged with sadness.

Carrie felt faint, but she managed to answer quietly.

"I didn't know that I was supposed to be there. I didn't know I was meant to be waiting for your flight." She felt her knees giving way and she clutched at the door frame.

Paul was still furious.

"Don't give me that Carrie. I've known that you had some kind of agreement with Dan for years. He just dropped me off at the end of the road, told me while we were getting here that he gave you a letter three years ago explaining everything. He was sure that you would stand by what he asked you. But you didn't…" Paul trailed off helplessly.

Carrie's vision cleared slightly, but she was still very confused. Her voice trembled as she spoke.

"But he didn't give me any letter Paul. He hasn't asked me to do anything. I haven't seen or heard a thing from him in nearly three years. If he sent a letter, it must have been lost in the post. I swear Paul, I haven't received a thing from him in all the time you have been away." Carrie had tears of desperation in her eyes.

Lisa jumped in.

"And Carrie thought, because Daniel never made a move on her before you both left, she thought that he must be gay. That's what that vile reporter thought too. That's why she asked those ridiculous questions."

Paul looked completely dumbfounded.

"Gay! Daniel gay? Have you gone completely mad? He's probably the least gay man I know. Just because a guy doesn't fool a round or play the field, doesn't mean that he's gay, but whatever that evil cow insinuated or whatever Carrie thought, it doesn't explain why Carrie didn't get the letter. Dan said he'd given it to you, not sent it.

Jim found his way out from behind the door. He

209

couldn't look at either Carrie or Paul. He looked down at the floor as he stammered.

"I...I...err, I think I may have to make a confession." There was stunned silence as everyone looked over at him. He continued nervously. "Daniel gave a letter to me when you both came round the night you left for Atlanta, just before Carrie was due home from that first tour. He was telling me about the cheap plane tickets going out from Birmingham and that he wouldn't be able to come to her welcome home party. He didn't know if he'd get time to see Carrie before he flew so he asked me to pass it on." His face was rapidly turning crimson and Carrie heard her mother whisper.

"Oh no! What have you gone and done now Jim?"

Jim was still spluttering. He turned to his wife.

"I thought he was trying to make her go to America, Helen! I had every right not to give her the letter."

Carrie stood firmly now. She faced her father.

"You have to hope and pray that you still have it dad, or I swear to God that there is going to be a murder in this family." Her tone would have splintered solid granite.

Jim moved quickly to the sideboard and rummaged right at the back of a drawer, for what felt like an eternity. He pulled out a dusty, crumpled envelope. It was addressed to Carrie in bold black writing. Carrie snatched it from his hand and tore it open.

Three closely written sheets were in her hand.
She began to cry at the first line.

Carrie, I love you.
There! I've said it at last. It's so simple on paper.
I love you. See, easy.

I have wanted to say these words to you so many times over the last few weeks, over the last few years really. I've known that I wanted to be with you since I was about twelve. You had just come up to the senior school and you looked just so cute in your new uniform. I hadn't realized how much I had missed walking to school with you after I left the Juniors, but suddenly I just knew that I had. I was so happy every time I saw you coming along the road towards me.

Then earlier this year, when I was filling in the application forms for Atlanta, it all hit me like a brick between the eyes. I felt physically sick as I posted the application. I wasn't going to see you for three years! And then I knew it was way more than just missing walking along a road with you. I should have told you the truth then, but I just couldn't, and now I've gone and left it too late. All those years of walking right beside you, all the times I could have said something about how I feel. I can't believe how stupid I've been.

And I couldn't tell you just as you are about to embark on a fabulous dancing career and I am about to leave you for three years. What a fool eh?

I'm only writing this now because I'm sure you feel the same about me. Carrie, I swear I could hear your heart beating every time I was near you. And the gasps of pain, that were no such thing. I could see the pulse in your throat leaping endlessly. God! I so wanted to kiss it. And when your lips trembled, I just wanted to cover them with mine. The few times I touched your bare skin were pure torture. And when you cried and I held you because you felt lonely! I can barely write this now for the feelings that are burning through my body.

I've had to keep everything back from you and I don't know how I've managed it, but I can't take you from your family or your education or your dancing. Sixteen is way too young to give everything up. I know I may make it out in the States, but I may not either. I can't take the risk of asking you to come with me. It wouldn't be fair.

Carrie, I want you to do something for me. I want you to wait for me. I know I have no right to ask, but please believe me when I say that I know I will only ever love you and that I will come back for you. The way things are going with your dancing, you probably won't even notice that I'm gone, so three years will be easy for you.

I'm not going to contact you at all while I'm gone. I can't. If I see you, or even hear you, I will be lost completely. It's hard enough knowing I am leaving a day early and I can't even tell you all this. You'll cry again and then I will have to stay. I can't do that. I have of make a go of this for us.

When my course is finished and I'm on my way home, I'll ask Paul to call. He'll leave you the flight date and number. I'm too scared to do it myself in case I have this all wrong. I'm praying that I don't. If you're at the airport, I'll know that you have waited for me and that you love me and want me as much as I love and want you.

I so need you to wait for me.

Please be there Carrie.

Daniel

P.S. I've written out enough "I love you's" for you to have at least one for every day that I'm gone.

P.P.S. Don't show this to your dad, I would hate for him to think I'm soft.

P.P.P.S. Sorry about the doughnuts and the chewing gum and the foam. I only did it because I thought you might like me more if I could protect you from the so called 'School bully.'

The next pages were covered in hundreds of tiny "I love you's"

Carrie was sobbing and laughing into the letter.

The paper was becoming damp as she cried.

Helen had been reading over Carrie's shoulder. She looked up at her husband with stricken eyes.

"Oh Jim! How could you? Why didn't you give this to her?"

Jim's shoulders were slumped, his face an odd shade of grey. He had been reading the letter too.

"Okay, I admit it. I was wrong about him." His face blanched as he re-read parts of the letter. "Completely and utterly wrong. He's a really nice kid, decent and everything, but I didn't know that at the time. I just thought he was only after one thing. You were at least." His tone accused Paul, but then he saw Lisa standing beside her husband in her fabulous designer outfit with a happy, well fed, well dressed Tommy in her arms and he glanced up at Paul, who shot back a look of pure venom. "Well, I thought you were only after one thing. I was obviously wrong about that too. For God's sake Helen, look at them!" Jim shouted desperately. "They're like bloody giants. Any father would feel the same! I was scared for her!"

Paul pulled himself up to his tallest, his head narrowly missing the ceiling. He squared his massive shoulders and bunched his fists at his sides as he loomed over Jim.

"Scared of what Mr. Denton?" The furious look on Paul's face told Jim that he should be very scared indeed.

He cowered back as Paul advanced on him and he spoke quickly when his back hit the wall.

"Okay. I was swayed by my own stupid prejudices. I know that being tall doesn't make you a predator. I was being a complete idiot. I'm really sorry." Jim's voice had gone up a couple of octaves.

Paul was still looming.

"How sorry?" He growled menacingly as he took another step forwards. The tips of his massive shoes touched Jim's much smaller ones.

Jim floundered around in his brain. He looked to Helen for help and met only her steely gaze. Suddenly inspiration came to him. He stood up straight again, a glint in his eye. He slid sideways, away from Paul's overpowering figure.

"Sorry enough to get Carrie a flight out of here right now. Where the hell is my credit card?" He began patting his pockets wildly. Helen turned and pulled his credit card from a drawer in the sideboard while Lisa took a business card from her handbag.

"That's British Airways first class direct line. Make the call Jim." Lisa's tone was like ice.

Helen found the telephone and passed it to her husband. He immediately shoved it back at Helen.

"You make the call Helen. I've got a better idea. Got your passport handy Carrie?" He barely waited for her to nod and grab up her handbag from the floor. "Right, Paul, you get on the blower to your mate, make

215

sure that he knows we're on our way." He gave Carrie a quick grin. "Come on then girl, let's see if we can get you there on time. Ring me when you know what flight you've booked." He yelled back at Helen as he ran out of the door towards the car

Chapter Fifteen
Heathrow Airport

"Shit, shit, shit!" Jim thumped the top of the steering wheel in frustration. "Bloody security! It's all that bastard Bin Laden's fault. We're not allowed up on the ramp. I'm sorry Carrie, love, I'm going to have to drop you here and let you run." He pulled the car over to the kerb. "You have that flight number? It's the only one going to Atlanta this afternoon so he must be getting on it. Call us when you get there." He leaned over to her and kissed her on the cheek.

Carrie had been sitting silently for the half twenty minute journey. She took one more look at her father, leaned over, gave him a quick forgiving squeeze, and then opened the car door.

"Thanks dad. If I manage to catch the flight I'll ring you." And then she was sprinting away across the front of the terminal building.

Daniel stood restlessly in the first class lounge bar looking up at the bank of television monitors. His flight was apparently going to leave on time, but no gate number had been given yet. He ordered a vodka and tonic and sat on a bar stool. He stood up again as he felt the hard plastic lump in the back pocket of his trousers. He grabbed the phone he had picked up from his old home and flung it on the bar. It looked very old fashioned against his brand new iphone and for a few seconds he wondered why he had even bothered to pick it up.

He had only called into the house after he had dropped Paul off, to see the old place one more time. He had bought it two years previously at way over the market value to enable his parents to move into their own separate homes and he had meant to put it on the market to resell.

He didn't realize, until he stepped through the door, that his parents had only taken their own belongings. His old room was like a time warp, still full of his teenage junk. His old phone had been lying on the bedside cabinet, exactly where he had left it three years previously.

He tapped at one or two of the fat buttons and then gave it up when he realized that the battery would have run out years ago.

He finished his vodka and swivelled in his seat to glance up at the departures screen again. Still nothing for his flight. He turned suddenly as someone spoke behind him.

"You want that charged?" The barman was speaking to him.

Daniel hesitated for a second, unsure of what he was talking about, then he saw the man nod at the old phone. He pushed it towards the barman as he picked up his empty glass. He turned it around in his fingers.

Drinking wasn't really his thing, but he felt the occasion merited it.

He had never felt so hollow in his life. In the three years he'd been away, it had never once occurred to him that Carrie didn't feel the same about him or, even worse, that she might have moved on. He nearly threw up the vodka again at the thought of her being with another man.

The barman was fiddling under the counter. He came up with a thin black wire and before Daniel could move, he had picked up the old telephone and plugged it in. He looked back up at Daniel.

"Lucky that one was a popular model Mr. Lewis, we've got a jack to fit. And would you like another drink while you're waiting? These old phones can take a while, even if we do have a super- fast connection."

Daniel nodded again and looked at the old phone. The screen was lit up with a soft green glow, but nothing showed on the face. He wondered for a mad moment if the left over credit would still be valid. Like the odd twenty quid mattered to him now that he had millions!

Daniel swallowed. All the millions in the world meant nothing to him right at this moment. He knew instantly that he would have given up every single thing he owned just to have Carrie there at his side.

The barman put his drink in front of him. Daniel sipped at it slowly and looked back up at the departures screen. His flight number was flashing with a gate number adjacent to it. He was about to down his drink in one go when the barman spoke again.

"No need to rush Sir. The gate is called a good forty minutes before takeoff. You might as well sit here and enjoy your drink in peace as go down there with the crowd. Give it ten minutes and your phone will have charged too." He started to polish some glasses.

Daniel nodded at the barman and sat back again. He stared to the old phone's green screen, wondering how he had read Carrie's body language so wrongly all that time ago. He had been so sure of her. He had been able to feel her heart beating beneath her ribs as he had helped her with the exercises. It had thundered more than when she came off the dance floor. He frowned as he began to wonder about his sports injury clinics. If he had totally misread a completely open young woman, maybe he wasn't so good at reading other people's signs either. He drummed his fingers on the bar as he watched the little yellow battery sign, now showing, fill and then empty again as the phone charged slowly.

Carrie raced to the check in desk and flung her reference number and passport at the clerk.

"Your luggage?" The young woman asked.

"None. I didn't bring any luggage." Carrie answered breathlessly.

The woman looked at her watch.

"Just as well. I was about to close the check in. You'll have to hurry to gate seventeen, it's closing in five minutes. Are you sure you wouldn't prefer to take the next flight? It's only a four hour wait and then you wouldn't have to run."

Carrie bobbed up and down impatiently, wishing the woman would just issue the boarding card, rather than waffling endlessly.

"No, it has to be this one. Please hurry." Carrie begged. The woman pulled out the printed boarding card at last and handed it to Carrie.

"You can go straight through to first class. Take the door on your right and you should get there a little quicker."

Carrie snatched the card from the woman's hand and dodged other passengers as she made for the first class lounge. The doors opened automatically and she was suddenly surrounded by luxury. She scanned around the lounge and then noticed a flashing light on a monitor, indicating that her gate number was closing. She sprinted towards the opposite exit, along the now deserted corridor and into another flight lounge. There were several gates with people milling about them. She ran onto gate seventeen.

The seating area was totally deserted. There was a short piece of twisted rope strung across the gangway to the plane. Carrie took another look up at the monitor. The sign flashed 'Gate Closed.' She stared at it for one more second and then pulled the twisted rope from its mooring.

A shrill bleeping immediately started up in the lounge and several people at the other gates looked in her direction. She barely glanced back at them before she was off down the gangway. Two turns later she could see the aeroplane door up ahead. It looked firmly closed. She began to run as she heard footsteps pounding behind her.

"Dan!" She yelled desperately at the plane door. "Daniel wait, I'm coming!" She scrambled a few strides nearer and then she was brought down hard from behind. Someone grabbed her around her waist and rugby tackled her to the ground.

"Ah ha! Got you!" The burly guard shouted triumphantly.

Carrie kicked out.

"Let me go you idiot. I have a ticket for that plane and I'm getting on it." She wriggled out of the man's grasp only to feel more arms on her, this time round her chest. A second guard clamped his arms around her torso and lifted her off the ground, swinging her round to face the direction from which she'd come.

"Not so fast, young lady. The gate closed five minutes ago. This is now a restricted area and that plane is about to leave. If you don't stop struggling I am going to have to use greater force and none of us would like that, would we?" He spoke through gritted teeth.

Carrie flung herself against the guards straining arms, kicking out furiously with her legs, and for just a second he lost his grip.

She was off in an instant, but she had only moved two paces when she saw, to her horror, that the plane door was no longer there. She ran to the now open ended corridor and stared out at the tarmac. The giant plane was already twenty meters away.

"Dan!" She screamed at it as she teetered on the edge of the thirty foot drop. "Dan, come back! I love you!" But it was way too late. The huge plane kept moving and Carrie, felt her legs begin to wobble, but she didn't have time to fall. The next moment she felt a hard metal tube sticking in the side of her head. She was about to turn and face it, when someone spoke to her in a voice that filled her with dread.

"One more move and we shoot. Now very slowly, put your hands behind your head and step back from the edge." She stepped back quickly. "Get down on the floor…NOW!" The man bellowed as Carrie hesitated for a fraction of a second.

Her knees felt so weak, she didn't have the strength to kneel slowly. One moment she was standing and the next her kneecaps hit the floor with a crack. Instantly she was pushed forwards onto her stomach, her hands were pulled behind her back and she felt cold steel encircle her wrists and pull tight.

She tried to lift her head to look forwards, to take a last glimpse of Daniel's plane but one of the guards put his foot on top of her head and held her down, while the other radioed in for back up.

Daniel stared in amazement at the screen of his old telephone. He had come to the men's room to wash his hands and face just before boarding his plane and had only looked at the screen of his old phone because it had bleeped unexpectedly at him. He had dried his hands carefully and looked again as the phone beeped repeatedly. Then he noticed the message on the tiny screen.

How many missed calls?!

Now he was gawping at the sheer volume of them. There were over a thousand, all from the same number. A number he recognised instantly. He backed into a cubicle and sat down hard on the toilet seat, completely dumbfounded. His finger shook as he dialled up voice mail and listened to the first message.

There was complete silence and then what sounded like a tiny sigh of breath. He moved to the next message, only to hear the same sound. He skipped seven of the messages and listened again. He nearly dropped the phone when he heard a gentle but familiar voice.

"I miss you Dan." It whispered.

He smiled for what felt the first time that day. He listened to the next five messages. They were all exactly the same. Carrie's soft tones filled his ears.

"I miss you Dan."

He skipped the next ten messages and listened once more. His hand gripped the phone reflexively and his heart thudded wildly as he heard.

"I love you Dan." This time the message was followed by a tiny frightened gasp. He looked at the call log and saw that there had been no calls for three days after this. The next message was the same, more confident now. No frightened gasp.

"I love you Dan."

He skipped a few more and then the next one had him gulping into the phone.

"I expect you've heard the news. I'm going to miss her but I'm really happy for Lisa and Paul. She'll be with you tomorrow evening…" She hesitated for a moment and then added quietly. "I wish it was me coming to meet you Daniel. I love you."

By the time he had skipped through to message number three hundred, Carrie was almost shouting.

"Hey Dan! I love you!" Her voice sounded happy and light.

The next one certainly wasn't. A very cross sounding Carrie said.

"So! Sabotaging my driving test eh! I will be talking to you about that one when you get home and you had better have some damned good excuse for what you have in your hand, and I don't mean the hand holding the bottle! Never the less," She had added primly. "I still love you Dan."

He grinned wildly, not really understanding what she meant, but realizing that he had put her off her test somehow.

The following message had him raising his eyebrows in surprise.

Danny? What the hell! His mind boggled at the name. *Giving up her day job? And 'Big arse'? What the hell was that all about?* He shook his head and looked to see when the last message had been left. It had only been left the night before.

226

He was almost too scared to listen. If she was going to tell him that she wasn't going to meet him, he didn't want to hear it.

He looked at the phone, as if he could see the message rather than hear her voice, and then he raised his finger slowly and touched the button.

There was a pause before Carrie spoke this time, almost as though she was frightened again, and then her voice came over loud and perfectly clear.

"Mum has just told me that you're coming home tomorrow. I hope I can see you, but if you're too busy and I don't manage to and if you ever get to listen to all these messages, you will probably realize something..." She paused and then said. "I love you Daniel." The message clicked off.

Daniel grinned stupidly as he stared at the phone. His iphone began buzzing in his other pocket. He took it out and looked at the screen. He tapped the icon to receive the text from Paul and laughed out loud as he read the words. They were all written in capitals as though Paul were shouting at him. He could almost hear his friend bellowing.

"DO NOT GET ON THE PLANE!!!!! ALL HER TWAT FATHER'S FAULT!!!!! SHE DIDN'T GET YOUR LETTER!   IF YOU ARE ON THE

227

PLANE, GET OFF NOW! CARRIE IS ON HER WAY! SHE LOVES YOU! :) "

Daniel leapt off the toilet seat and walked to the wash basin. He splashed water over his face again and then looked at himself in the mirror. His eyes were sparkling as brightly as flawless blue diamonds. He glanced at his watch and was surprised at how much time had passed as he had sat in the cubicle. He had missed his flight anyway. He wiped his face on the thick paper towel and marched out of the men's room.

He was surprised to see the first class lounge swarming with security police. The nearest officer whirled round to Daniel, his gun poised.

Daniel put his hands up automatically, but the officer lowered the gun immediately as he recognised the world famous American footballer.

"Didn't you hear the loud speakers, Mr. Lewis. We have been asking everyone to leave the area while we clear up this security problem."

"Problem?" Daniel really didn't care what the problem was, he just wanted to get out now. "If I can just leave, then I'll be out of your hair. I'm not catching my flight after all." He side stepped along the wall, but the next security guard stopped him.

"Best if you wait here now. We're just bringing her through. Stupid woman tried to get on a plane as it was about to leave. She breached the security barriers and all hell let loose. We think she's just another late passenger, but she's slightly hysterical and what with the terrorist thing, we can never be too sure. If you wouldn't mind standing back Sir, this will all be over in a jiffy." He pushed Daniel back behind him.

Daniel didn't bother resisting, he could see over the shorter man's shoulder easily. He stared curiously out to a small knot of officers who were half carrying, half pulling a young woman between them. Daniel's mouth fell open as he saw a mass of the darkest brown hair shining under the overhead lights. The guards moved quickly as it looked as though the woman was about to collapse. Her pale, tear stained face was visible for just a second. Daniel gasped and pushed out from behind the officer.

"Carrie." He whispered, full of shock and then he shouted as he found his voice once again. "Carrie!" And he moved forwards quickly.

The officer leapt round him to block his way. Daniel shoved the man aside with his shoulder as Carrie's head came up at the sound of his voice. The officer brought up his gun. Daniel stopped dead. He saw Carrie staring around like a frightened, wild animal, but she couldn't see past the wall of uniformed security men.

"Carrie! Over here! Get out of my way!" Daniel yelled as yet another security guard stepped in front of him. The man moved a fraction, unsure of what to do.

He had recognized Daniel immediately and knew that he was no terrorist.

And then Carrie caught sight of him. She stopped dead for a second, staring directly at him, her rose red lips parted and said his name silently. Then the guard immediately behind her shoved her roughly in the small of her back. She stumbled forwards, almost tripping as she lurched at the unexpected blow.

Daniel felt his whole body bristle, and then he noticed her arms were pulled behind her back, her wrists held by a set of handcuffs.

He cried out in rage as he saw her anguish.

"For God's sake let her go!" He shouted as he made to run forwards, only to be brought up short by the guard blocking his path for the third time.

The guard looked back at Carrie.

"Who? Her? Sorry Sir, no can do until we have a full security check done. It's probably going to be routine, but we do have to be sure."

Daniel looked down at the man. He appeared to have an extra set of stripes on his uniform. He quelled his fury, knowing that it would get him nowhere,

"Are you the senior officer here?" He asked in his most polite fashion. The man nodded fractionally. Daniel carried on. "I'm really sorry officer, but I think you have made a terrible mistake. That woman is Carrie Denton, the lead dancer for "Half Past Blue" and more recently for Milana on her world tour…" He paused as he saw Carrie's head turning to follow him as she was led away. He started after her as if in a dream and then said. "She also happens to be my girlfriend."

The guard looked up at Daniel again and then across to Carrie's retreating figure.

"Girlfriend! But we all thought you were…that reporter said that you…Oh, never mind." He spluttered to a halt as Daniel glowered at him, then he carried on. "Well, if she's your girlfriend, what in the Devil's name was she doing trying to board plane that was literally leaving the gate. Apart from anything else she could have been killed if she'd fallen from the gangway. And why aren't you together on the flight anyway?" He was walking behind Daniel, waving his men back as they stepped forwards to block his path.

Daniel glanced over his shoulder at the man who was almost jogging to keep up with his enormous stride.

"She didn't know that I changed my mind. We had a bit of a misunderstanding earlier today and I was going to leave, but I decided not to fly after all. I just went to the men's room to freshen up. I expect she was worried that we were separated. Please stop them and let her go. If she's in trouble for going through a gate, then fine, we can sort that out, but take her out of the handcuffs please. She's no danger to anyone." Daniel was about to force his way through the door into a security area, but the officer in charge put his hand on Daniel's shoulder and shook his head as he turned.

"I'm sorry Sir, but I'm afraid it's not going to be as simple as that. You didn't see what she did to one of my officers! His shins are black and blue. There's going to be an assault charge at the very least. You can wait here if you like, but I must inform you that incidents like this are taken very seriously indeed. I will take what you say into consideration, but I can't just let her go. Sit here Mr. Lewis. I'll let you know when and if she's free to go."

Chapter Sixteen
Midnight

"Surely they must have finished with her by now. How much longer can they keep her locked up like this?" Daniel was pacing along the front of the bar, watching the security doors through the small crowd of passengers that had been allowed back into the first class lounge.

"Haven't got a clue mate." Paul answered and he sipped at his beer. He had come along as moral support after Daniel had called him, bellowing down the phone about 'Police brutality' and 'civil rights.' "I think with a possible terrorist thing it's up to twenty-eight days...but I could be wrong." He added quickly as Daniel turned a deep purple and seemed to swell to double his normal size.

"But she only crossed a barrier, for God's sake. She hadn't even checked any luggage, and she didn't delay the plane. She hadn't even a hair grip on her let alone something as deadly as a nail file. They must know exactly who she is by now, and that she's no threat." Daniel suddenly stopped as the security door at the other side of the lounge opened at last.

The officer in charge came through and marched straight towards them. His face gave nothing away. He walked up to Daniel.

"Sorry to have kept you so long Sir, but these

checks do take their time. Well, it seems she's exactly who you said she was." He glanced up at Paul who was muttering sarcastically into his beer.

"And it took nearly nine hours to find that out? Don't you lot use the internet? Would have taken about five seconds on Google. No wonder you need twenty-eight days for anyone really suspicious." He shook his head in dismay.

The security guard narrowed his eyes and puffed out his chest as he stood very straight. It didn't look very impressive in comparison to Paul and Daniel's massive statures.

"You can mock Sir, but we find it best to be thorough."

Daniel broke in, not wanting an argument to start.

"What about the assault on your officer? Are you going to charge her?"

The man shook his head.

"My man decided not to press charges. He says he's willing to put up with a few bruises in view of the er…unusual circumstances."

Daniel leaned forwards eagerly.

"So can she leave now? We've been waiting a long time and I really need to see her." There was something desperate in his tone and the guard deflated slightly.

"Yes, after reading that letter you sent to her, I

can imagine you do…Very passionate, I must say." He waggled his eyebrows. "It's no wonder she wanted to get on that plane so desperately." He stopped as Daniel turned a deep shade of red, and hurried on, not wanting to embarrass him further. "Well, we have a couple of conditions before we let her go."

"Anything!" Daniel was about to get onto his knees and beg for her to be released.

The officer smiled slightly.

"Do you think you two can take a few minutes to give my men a couple of autographs?" Daniel was already reaching for his pen. "And do you think you could try and keep your girlfriend under control from now on? Your letters obviously make her far too excitable. It might be best if you stick to talking rather than writing. I don't want to have to arrest her formally. I already have enough paperwork to last a month with this little incident. Anything worse and I'm going to be seriously annoyed." He smiled as he gave a hand signal to the security guard positioned at the door.

A few minutes later Carrie stepped out into the first class lounge. Her hair was dishevelled, skin pale and delicate from crying. She was rubbing her wrists as she looked round frantically.

And then her eyes met Daniel's. She blinked as though clearing her vision, then her eyes rolled slightly and her body drooped.

She looked as though she was about to collapse

as she stared at him.

He saw her stagger just one tiny pace towards him, and then he was off. He launched himself across the lounge, hurtling past amazed travellers, leaving them all standing wide eyed in his wake.

"Christ! He's fast!" The officer spoke to Paul, as Daniel vaulted over a row of chairs, and dodged a group of passengers that blocked his path.

Paul nodded and raised an eyebrow as he finished his beer in one last gulp.

"Yup. Fastest in the squad." He licked his lips. "Ah! Nothing like English beer! One thing I really missed." He glanced towards Daniel, who was just skidding to a stop in front of Carrie. "He'd leave them for dead if he ever went in for the hundred meters in the Olympics, the hurdles too, by the looks of the way he jumped those chairs. Well, if you don't mind, I think I'm going to get back to my wife and son. They'll be missing me. I only came along to give the sentimental fool a bit of moral support, but by the looks of it, I don't think Dan is going to need me for the next few days." He gave the guard a hefty slap on the back that sent him reeling into the nearest barstool, and then he strolled out of the doors.

Daniel stood in front of Carrie, breathing deeply. He didn't know whether to grab her to him, or kiss her passionately, or scoop her up and swing her round.

Instead he stood watching her rub her wrists. He lifted his hand and took one of hers, turning it gently in his huge palm, massaging the redness with the pad of his thumb. He heard her swallow and glanced into her slate grey eyes. She was staring right back at him.

"You didn't get on the plane." She said hoarsely, a slow tear running down her cheek.

He shook his head and gulped noisily. He cleared his throat.

"No. I received your message in time. Or messages, I should say. You've left rather a lot of them. I didn't listen to them all, but I think I got the gist of what you meant."

Carrie frowned, not understanding what he was talking about. Daniel pulled the old mobile from his inside pocket and held it up. She recognized it immediately, noticed the number of messages on it and flushed to the roots of her hair.

"Oh! Where did you find that?" She stammered as she realized that nearly three years' worth of, "I love you Dan." were now on open display.

Daniel shrugged and slipped it back in his pocket.

"At home. My parent's old home that is. Don't you remember. I forgot it when Paul and I left for Birmingham three years ago. We were in such a hurry to see you and Lisa before we caught our flight that night, we decided not to go back for it. I just left it behind. It was still on my bedside cabinet when I went to look at the house after that damned interview earlier today. I bought the house a couple of years back, so my parents could sort themselves out. They're separated now, but so much happier. It was a bit of a shock to find that they left my room exactly as it was three years ago. I couldn't believe it. Like some kind of teenage time warp. They even left my stinking old trainers. I don't know what made me pick the phone up, probably something to do with the fact that it was the only thing that would fit in my pocket, I suppose. The barman in here charged it for me while I was waiting for my flight." His voice was barely a whisper. "Your wrists look sore Carrie, have they only just let you out of those cuffs?" He changed the subject.

She shook her head and looked down.

"A couple of hours ago, but I was too afraid to move. My arms are as stiff as boards. I'm not often still for that long."

Daniel began to move his warm hands slowly up her arms towards her shoulders, sending shivers of pleasure through her slender frame.

"No, I can imagine you're always on the go." He rubbed the top of her arms with his fingertips and leaned in a fraction closer to her.

Carrie could feel her heart pounding inside her ribcage as she felt the heat coming from his body.

He slipped a long finger under her chin.

"I got your letter." She nearly choked as she looked up into his bluer than blue eyes. "It was delivered this afternoon. Better late than never I suppose…Dad thought he was doing the best thing for me." She didn't know what else to say.

Daniel nodded once and then smiled grimly.

"Paul told me everything while we were waiting. I am going to have some serious words with your father about that. He gave me a solemn promise that he would give you that envelope as soon as you were home from that tour." He lifted her chin further and looked down into her slate grey eyes. They were dark and mysterious and he wanted to keep looking into them forever.

There was a slight crease across his forehead and Carrie raised her hand to trace her finger along it. Daniel closed his eyes as her touch seared his skin and he let out a deep groan of longing.

He opened his eyes again immediately as he heard Carrie take in a painful breath. She dropped her hand back to her side. Her arm hung limply for a moment, then she shook it gently.

"Sorry, I've been so cramped up in that room for the last few hours, my shoulder has gone stiff."

Daniel stepped back a fraction and looked quizzically at her.

"Yes, it probably would, you never really recover fully from an injury like that. Would some exercises help? Come on now, deep breath in and out, and slowly raise your arms." His voice flowed over her and she closed her eyes as he intoned the familiar instructions. "Now open them wide and roll your neck gently. Another breath in, no don't let it out yet." There was a short pause. Carrie kept her eyes shut and smiled gently as she felt his breath waft over her. "Now, let your breath go and reach up again, higher, go on, all the way or it won't work, now clasp your hands together and reach forwards." She smiled again as she felt the brush of his hair on the tender skin inside her elbow as he ducked his head under the arch she had made with her arms. "And bring your arms down, stretch out your fingers, that's right, bend your elbows a little." She could feel his hair in her hands now and the next second she was running her fingertips through the thick dark strands at the back of his neck, then she was pulling his head down to hers.

He groaned again, the sound rumbling in his massive chest as she felt his huge hands encircle her face. His words whispered over her, a mere breath away from her lips. "God Carrie! You are a complete natural at this…" He prolonged the moment, his breath coming in giant pulls. "I have missed you so much."

And then his lips touched hers, gently, experimentally at first, then with an edge of desperation.

Fire raged through her whole body as her lips

parted, inviting him to taste her.

He needed no more encouragement. He slanted his mouth, his tongue running along her teeth, tasting her sweet flavour, darting into her delicious mouth. He was moving his hands from her face to her body, pulling her into him, lifting her, clasping her as if he were a drowning man thrown a life line.

He could hear his own pulse banging in his ears, nearly deafening him as he held on to the only thing that would ever matter to him for the rest of his life.

And then Carrie pulled away slightly, sliding down his body as her feet slipped back to the floor. Her lips were moist and throbbing, reddened by his passion, almost bruised from his crushing kiss, but she was smiling widely, her face now crimson.

Daniel stared down at her. He wanted so much more, he wanted all of her. Three years was too long for a Saint to wait, let alone a red blooded footballer. He bent to kiss her again, but stopped as he suddenly realized that the deafening roar he could hear wasn't just his own blood surging round his body or his pulse throbbing violently in his head. It was happening all around him. His eyes flicked over Carrie's beautiful face once more and then he glanced up to see a crowd of people, passengers and security guards, all standing round, staring at them, cheering and clapping wildly.

He stood back, grinning sheepishly, and made a small bow. The crowd gave a collective laugh and started talking again as they turned and went back to their own business.

Carrie laughed too. Her heart was soaring in her chest as Daniel took her arm. He looked over the crowd and saw the exit light flashing gently. He kissed her quickly again, brushing his cheek against hers as he indicated the exit.

She touched her tingling skin.

"You need a shave." She said gently. "You needed one the last time I saw you."

Daniel rubbed his hand over his face, feeling the hours old stubble.

"God! The last time I saw you…That feels so long ago. It was so long ago. I don't know how I stopped myself taking you there and then on that terrace by the lake. That night was so beautiful, I've lived on the feeling of you sleeping in my arms for nearly the last three years. Come on, I'm not too sure about doing this sort of thing with such an enthusiastic audience in attendance. I need to be with you in private. Let's get out of here." He pulled her towards the door as he noticed one or two of the other passengers still watching them with interest.

Carrie giggled.

"I should have thought that you of all people would be used to the attention. After all, it's not as though you haven't been in the limelight. You were picked for the team almost as soon as you arrived in

Atlanta."

Daniel put his arm protectively around her shoulder, pulling her to him as they struggled through the crowded terminal building.

"Huh! All I've been doing is chucking a ball about and barging through a crowd of sweaty blokes. It's not that hard. And I've never asked for the attention. In fact, apart from when trying to earn a few quid, I've done my utmost to avoid it." He stopped for just a moment as two young boys, aged about eleven and thirteen came charging up in front of them, blocking their way, their faces lit up with rapt expressions. A man was hustling behind them, dragging luggage and carrying a tiny sleeping baby like a papoose. He had obviously heard Daniel's last words.

"Sorry! Sorry! They don't mean to be a nuisance." His tone was apologetic. "Come along boys." He hefted his bag onto his shoulder, narrowly avoiding the baby as he grabbed his two sons by the backs of their t-shirts. "Leave Mr. Lewis alone. He's just back from America and he won't want to be bothered by you two."

There were joint howls of indignation. One of the boys looked up at his father with a strange expression on his face.

"Who's Mr. Lewis dad? It's Carrie Denton's autograph we want. She's hot! Phwarr! And she's a really famous dancer. She was with Half Past Blue, and

Milana!" His words came spilling out as he looked as though it was something that the whole world should know.

Carrie's jaw dropped and then she laughed out loud as Daniel rolled his eyes and passed his poised pen over to her. She signed their books willingly and passed them back. They insisted on kisses too. She gave them both a small peck on the cheek, then they turned their flaming cheeks back to their smiling father, who waved a thanks. The boys disappeared into the crowd again and Daniel looked down at Carrie, his eyebrows raised.

"Is that something I should be worried about? I mean, do I have a lot of rival fans to beat off?"

Carrie shrugged as they walked out of the terminal building.

"Probably not as many as are hanging onto your coat tails. Actually that's the first time anything like that has ever happened to me. Fans only ever focus on the star so we dancers aren't normally noticed. I didn't even know anyone knew my name. I can't believe they recognized me, I look a complete wreck. They must have been very keen." They had reached the taxi rank.

Daniel turned to her.

"You don't look a wreck. You look completely perfect." He bent his head to kiss her again, but was brought up short by loud honking from the waiting taxi driver. Daniel opened the car door as the driver

244

apologized.

"Sorry mate, but the other drivers get annoyed if anyone hangs around. Where to?"

Carrie looked up at Daniel and then ducked inside the cab as he ushered her forwards.

"Where are we going to go? I feel completely washed out and I'm desperate for a shower, but I certainly don't want to home yet. Dad will be like the Spanish Inquisition."

Daniel held the car door open and bent almost double as he followed her inside. He sat down beside Carrie, his long legs stretching out and filling most of the space in the back of the car. He sighed deeply as he relaxed.

"I hate to say this Carrie, but I think I might be quite happy to subject your father to a few of their methods if I see him right now, and that's probably not the best way to start getting on with my future Father in Law." He leaned forwards and ignored Carrie's intake of breath as he spoke to the cab driver. "Felton Hall, near Windsor, do you know it? I can give you the postcode if you need it." He was answered with a shake of his head.

"No, you're all right Sir. I know the place, big old Georgian gaffe with a wall right the way around it. Backs onto Windsor Great Park. Used to be a Hotel, but it closed last year for a refit. I didn't realize it had reopened. Will you need picking up in the morning

245

Sir? I'm available anytime from seven onwards. With most of these fancy places I can arrange for a return journey if you require." The taxi driver was trying to be helpful.

Daniel looked back at Carrie who was now curled into the corner of the seat. She was staring back at him, her dark eyes wide with curiosity.

"Yeah, Okay, why not? I'll book another journey, but not in the morning, thanks." He smiled widely. "The Hall is a private residence now, so can you postpone the ride for about two months. I won't need you until the rugby season starts. I don't want to be interrupted before then." Daniel reached round behind him and began to pull up the privacy screen. "You can take me to my first game. I'll even get you a ticket." He heard the man laugh in delight just before he clipped the dense black material in place and switched off the intercom.

Daniel glanced at Carrie's puzzled expression and began to explain. "I may have been quite happy living in Atlanta with Paul and Lisa for the last three years, but I did want us to have our own home too. Not my parent's place either. I only bought that so they could get out. I don't particularly want to go there, too many unhappy memories. And it's probably a bit too close to your father for comfort at the moment." He waited as Carrie rolled her eyes in exasperation at her father. "I had an agent buy Felton Hall for us with some of the money I've earned. I've not had time to go there yet but it looks fantastic from the portfolio, so I'm hoping you'll like it. Actually I'm hoping I like it. There's a small staff who have been getting the place ready for us. I'd kind of assumed you would be with me too." Daniel sat back in his seat and pulled Carrie into his arms, unable to wait a moment longer. His breath was hot at her throat as he leaned in to nuzzle at her neck and then he lifted his head, stared into her dark grey eyes for a moment longer, then slanted his lips across hers as he kissed her.

They were completely breathless when they parted.

Carrie gasped out her words as she gulped in air.

"Two months then. Don't you want to see anybody at all during that time? Not even your old friends, I mean, what about Paul, won't you miss him at the very least?" Carrie asked quietly as his lips began brushing hers yet again.

Daniel sat back half an inch.

"Paul? Why the devil would I want to see Paul? I've seen him practically every day for the last…well, all my life actually. I think I can manage two months without him." He moved in again, but Carrie held up her hand, suddenly serious now.

"But what about training? You'll need the exercise to keep your fitness up. You can't let the England side down."

247

Daniel rolled his eyes.

"Shut up Carrie, and sod the rugby for a while. I'll get back to serious training later. I've been waiting for three years to be able to tell you I love you to your face, and there's a whole lot more I've been waiting to do with the rest of you too. I'm pretty sure I'm going to get all the physical activity I need." A strange rumble began somewhere deep in his chest.

Carrie giggled madly and flung her arms around his neck.

"God! How did I ever come to the conclusion you were gay! Okay, let's see if Atlanta's best excuse for a football player can make his first touchdown in the U.K." She looked down at her watch. "Maybe before two o'clock." And before he could reply, she pulled his lips onto hers.

Daniel moved away after only a few seconds. His hands were around her waist, tugging gently at her shirt as his eyes feasted over her for a second longer, and then he flipped the intercom on again.

"Hey, driver? You think you can get us there within twenty minutes for an extra ticket?" He glanced at his watch and then back at Carrie. He caught a glimpse of pale skin at her waistline. She was almost shimmering in the moonlight as it spilled through the cab window.

Daniel gulped and then almost growled. "Make that two sets of tickets if you can get us there in ten."

He didn't need to wait for an answer. He felt himself being pushed back into his seat as the driver hooted his horn at some unseen road hog and the cab leapt forwards, accelerating wildly into the night.

Chapter Seventeen
September 3rd 2010

"Got everything? Pen, note book, laptop, lunch?" Daniel was peering into Carrie's bag.

She pushed him out of the way and fastened the buckle.

"Yes, I packed everything, stop worrying. You're worse than my father." She moved to lift the bag to her shoulder.

He took the bag from her and looked down at her. She was wearing snuggly fitting denim jeans and white t-shirt. She looked utterly adorable and he feasted his eyes on her.

Carrie tried to take her bag back from him but he held it just out of her reach. She put her hands on her hips and stared at him.

He was still wearing his dark blue, silk dressing gown, the intense colour highlighting his beautiful blue eyes as he gazed at her. He had only climbed out of bed when he realized that he couldn't tempt her into not going to university.

He was suddenly puffing out his cheeks.

"I can't believe you're going to fresher's week! I wish I was coming with you. I'm not sure I trust all those young studs around you. I know what it was like when Paul and I first enrolled at Atlanta." Daniel reached out and touched her cheek.

250

She turned and kissed his fingers.

"Don't be silly Dan. You weren't tempted, so why do you think I will be? How could I possibly be attracted by anyone else but you, and it's not like I'm even leaving you for long. Not like the three ghastly years you put me through, I may add. I should have thought that I had well and truly proven that I don't want anyone else. I waited for you when I didn't even know I was meant to." She reached up and kissed him gently on the lips.

He groaned longingly.

"I know, I know and I love you even more for it, but do you really have to go now. I mean, I can still set you up in a studio without you having to bother with the degree. I won't mind if you don't have one. It's not like I'm going to check your C.V. or anything" He put his hands around her waist and tugged her body close to him.

Carrie frowned.

"Well, now you tell me! But no, I really want to do this Dan. I will be able to give much better advice if I'm properly trained. I want to know exactly what I'm doing, not just look as though I know exactly what I'm doing. Come on, you know it makes sense." She tried to wriggle out of his arms, but he held her firmly against him. She buried her head in his chest in defeat.

He rested his chin on the top of her head.

"I know, but I still don't want you to go. We've

not been apart at all these last two months and I still don't feel as though we've made up for those three years apart. It's going to be awful with you gone. I'm going to be so lonely." He grumbled into her hair.

Carrie nodded into his huge chest, almost swept away by his emotions. She replayed the two months in her mind and came up gasping for breath.

Their first night together had been incredible. After her dreadful experience at the airport, they had arrived at the fabulous Hall barely able to keep their hands off one another. Daniel had immediately dismissed the staff for the night and they had spent several precious minutes trying to find their bedroom.

He had undressed her carefully and then led her to the beautiful en-suite bathroom. They had showered together, touching each other's naked bodies for the first time, feeling their desires soar as the warm water cascaded over them.

Then Daniel had washed her hair, soaping away the traumas of the day, before eventually wrapping her in the softest towel and carrying her back to the enormous bed.

There had been just a few moments of embarrassment as he lay down beside her and quietly confessed that he had never made love to anyone before. Carrie had buried her head in his huge expanse of chest and, as he held her tightly, she confirmed what he already knew. She was a virgin too.

A few moments later, he had fumbled in a bedside drawer for a condom, but Carrie had put her hand over his, explaining quietly that, due to the unpredictable travelling arrangements and unreliable facilities on tours, she had been using the pill for years.

And then all embarrassment disappeared as they had let their bodies tell them what to do. Their limbs entwined and their kisses became deeper. He had been so gentle, so patient, as he made her his own. And so intensely passionate when, much later, she was gasping out his name in uncontrolled abandon, as they had peaked together. They had made love until dawn, over and over, three years of pent up emotions and desires, exploding with a ferocity unimaginable in even their wildest dreams.

Then they had slept for hours in each other's arms, only waking when their bodies told them they needed each other even more.

And every time since had been even better than the last.

A warm, tingling shot through her whole body at the thoughts that flooded her head. She tried to control her breathing, but she couldn't control her heart. She felt it pounding against her ribcage and she had to take a deep breath before speaking.

"I know. It's been the best two months of my

life. I never thought I could love you more than I did, but with everything else too. Oh Dan, don't make me think of it or I won't be able to walk out of the door." She wriggled some more as his hands began moving slowly down her back. They stopped at the base of her spine. He loosened his grip a fraction and she tipped her head back to look into his beautiful blue eyes.

He grumbled.

"That's the whole point Carrie. I don't want you to leave me. I'm perfectly happy to spend the day in bed with you again, and tomorrow too, and the day after that." He was grinning wickedly and she shivered with pleasure.

"Cut it out Dan. I know it's going to be difficult, but you have to be at training later this week anyway or they'll drop you from the squad. Paul is expecting you to pick him up too, so we might as well make this separation now rather than later." She pulled away from him at last.

He looked almost sulky as he replied.

"Okay, I understand, but I really wish you weren't going for so long. I'm going to be utterly deprived by the time I see you again. I'm only glad that you decided to drop the physiotherapy and stick with the basic sports injury training. It's the fast track course that you're taking, so it's only going to be for a year fulltime, thank goodness. I couldn't stand it any longer than that."

Carrie put her head down.

"No, me either. I'd rather be working with you every day, but this will be better for the future and you were always going on about getting a good education before you settled down. I'm only practising what you preached."

"Huh! Wish I'd kept my mouth shut now. I didn't know I was going to make millions at the time, or I wouldn't have bothered going on about it so much." He sounded almost defeated.

Carrie sighed deeply.

"Try and understand Daniel. Look at it from my point of view. They're your millions, not mine. I worked flat out for three years and didn't make a penny doing what I loved. I just about survived on the money I earned. I do have my pride if nothing else. Unless you want me going away for months on end touring for the next ten years, it's going to have to be this. I don't have any other choice."

Daniel smiled down at her and flicked her hair back from her face.

"Idiot. They're our millions. I couldn't have done any of it if you hadn't been there waiting for me. Even if you didn't know that you were meant to be waiting for me. You know, I don't think I'll ever be able to get over that. I don't know whether it was love or blind faith that made you wait all that time for me. I put absolutely everything into my work in Atlanta for us because I thought you had received my letter and knew how I felt. Thank God it just happened to work out alright anyway, so don't be doing this just because of the money."

She searched his eyes.

"I'm not doing this for the money. I'm doing this because I love dancing and I want to set up the studio with the clinic running along side it. My old colleague Oliver has agreed to take some of the dance classes now that I've managed to catch up with him and Jess is on board too. We don't know a single dancer that doesn't have painful injuries. They have knees that niggle, shoulders that crunch horribly, and ankles that click like they're out of joint. We're all decrepit by the time we're thirty. And we need help badly. This is going to be a fabulous venture. And Lisa is looking forward to joining the project too. She's going to be coming in part time. Tommy will be just starting pre-school soon so it'll be perfect timing for her and for me. Don't make me feel bad about leaving you, please Daniel."

His shoulders slumped in resignation.

"Okay, okay, leave me if you must, but I don't know what I'm going to do while you're gone. Don't be surprised if you return to find a raving lunatic chomping at the tapestries by the time you get home again. I'm going to need a massive project to keep me occupied."

She smiled indulgently at him.

"Okay, tell you what. The course finishes in late June. You do some searching on the internet and maybe we can have an early summer holiday. You'll be finishing the rugby season at the same time so organizing somewhere really nice will give you something to get your teeth into."

Daniel looked slightly happier. He quirked his lips up at her.

"Alright, I'll do it, I'll see what's going, but I want it to be somewhere special. Somewhere I've never been in real life. Like Rome maybe?"

She laughed lightly.

"You've been listening to those messages again." She accused him. "But yes, Rome was lovely. I'd love to be there with you for real this time, not watching you on the television." Carrie picked up her bag again.

He started walking towards the lounge. His bare feet sank into the thick carpet and he picked up his ipad before he slid onto the settee.

Carrie watched him as he moved his long fingers over the screen. His dressing gown had fallen open slightly and she could see a knot of tight muscles running across his chest and stomach. She began growing hot all over as she noticed the tangle of dark hair, pointing downwards, just below his navel.

He glanced up as he felt her eyes on him. He grinned and let the dressing gown fall open slightly more.

Carrie rolled her eyes and groaned, partly in longing, partly in frustration.

"Okay. That's enough of that sort of thing. I'm going."

He waved his hand dismissively.

"Alright, leave me, go off on your blasted course and leave me here pining for you. I'll book the holiday for June, but it won't be the same without you around." He pulled his best puppy dog expression. She walked over to the settee and bent to kiss him.

It lasted longer than she had anticipated and she was breathless by the time she stood back up.

"Tell you what." He looked up at her solemnly. "Would it make you change your mind about going to university if we made the holiday our honeymoon?"

Carrie gasped and stepped back.

"Daniel Lewis! That is the worst excuse for a proposal that I have ever heard, and no it won't make me change my mind about university." She smiled shyly at his crestfallen expression and added. "But if the offer's still open, yes I will marry you."

Daniel laughed delightedly.

"Excellent. I'll hold you to that, June it is. Go on then." He waved his hand at her again. "Leave me, get going. I'll have it all sorted out by the time you get back, the wedding included."

Carrie shook her head.

"There is no way you are going to have a wedding and a honeymoon sorted out by three o'clock this afternoon. There aren't any lectures today, it's just a saying hello sort of thing."

Daniel looked up from the screen.

"Huh, in that case don't say hello to too many people and you can be back even earlier. Are you walking or taking the car?"

"Car today, but I'll see how the parking is. Might be a nightmare. Should be back sooner than three if I'm driving. Do you think you can keep yourself from chomping on the tapestries until then." She grinned at him.

"I will do my very best. Thank goodness there's a course running locally. I would have gone completely mad if you had to go away. I'll expect you just after three, but if you're any later I won't be responsible for my actions." He suddenly put the ipad down and stood up. He walked over to her, letting the dressing gown fall completely open. He pulled her into his arms again, his hot, hard body warming her through her clothes. "You'd better get going Carrie, or I'm not going to be responsible for my actions right now." He kissed her tenderly.

She let him taste her mouth and then she stepped back and turned to the door.

"See you in about four hours then, and I promise you, I won't want you to be responsible for your actions when I get home."

He let her go.

"Good. I'm going to hold you to that, and just as a reminder, and only so that you don't forget me while you're saying hello to all these other students." He rummaged in his dressing gown pocket and lifted out a tiny box. "I want you to have this." He opened the box and Carrie gasped as the huge diamond glinted a million sparkles around the room. He picked the ring out of the velvet and lifted her left hand. The platinum band slipped perfectly onto her finger.

Carrie could barely speak.

"Dan, it's…I can't…I don't…" She floundered as the fabulous diamond glinted in the light. "It's so beautiful. Thank you." She whispered eventually.

Daniel put his finger over her lips and stared into her eyes.

"Shh, it's nothing. Just a small thank you for waiting for me, and a tiny token of my undying love." He shoved her towards the door. "Now go on woman, or you're going to be late. I don't want to hear that you were given a detention on your first day."

Carrie stopped in the doorway. Something he had said just reminded her.

"Detention? What? Like the one you tried to get me out of three years ago. For the silly string incident."

Daniel grinned.

"I seem to remember getting it cut to fifteen

minutes on the promise that I'd help you clear it all up."

Carrie shook her head and laughed.

"Yeah, well that might mean more if it hadn't been you that gave me the detention in the first place. And now that you remind me, there were the doughnuts and the chewing gum too."

Daniel flicked his hand dismissively at her.

"Serves you right for being so unobservant. If you'd fallen into my arms at that first incident we may not have had to wait three years. I think you still owe me for the torture."

She grinned at him again.

"Well just so you know, I don't have any money left so unless you're going to let me off the fine, I'll have to pay you in kind."

Daniel growled again.

"Good. The first payment is going to start at about two minutes past three this afternoon, and I don't take cash or credit, so make sure you're not late."

She nodded and then had an idea.

"Maybe I won't take the car. If I walk, you can come over and walk me home, just like we used to. I missed it the last couple of years at college. That way you can protect me from all the young studs and the bullies at the same time."

Daniel's expression brightened.

"Okay, you're on. I'll be right outside at three, so

don't be late."

Carrie walked out of the door and closed it behind her. She moved quickly down the hall and out onto the long drive before she took her mobile phone out of her pocket. She dialled Daniel's number. He answered on the first ring.

"Hi, have you forgotten something?"

She turned round on the driveway and looked back to where she could see him staring at her anxiously from out of one of the tall drawing room windows. She waved at him.

"It's nothing important, I just wanted to tell you something." She paused for a breath.

"What? What's wrong?" He sounded worried and she could see his eyebrows forming a solid black line across his forehead.

She started walking backwards as if she didn't want to lose sight of him ever again. Then she waved once more and whispered down the phone.

"Oh, it's nothing much. I just wanted you to know something…"

"What?" He sounded even more on edge as he stared out of the window.

She laughed into the phone and then clicked it off. She whirled around and around as he watched, her, arms open wide as she spun wildly.

Then she yelled out, as loudly as she could, for the whole world to hear.

"I LOVE YOU DANIEL!"

The End

Also Available from

amazon.co.uk and amazon.com

by

Jackie Williams

A Perfect Summer

A lifetime of pain and terror wiped out by one perfect summer of love.

Running Scarred

One man's fight for love, against the demons threatening to keep him running scarred for far too long.

Delicious Desires

A delicious desire for one man could become the love of his life's destruction.

Treasured Dreams

Could a thirteen year old girl's diary have really sealed the fate of her entire family.

Tinted Lenses

She's a photographer's dream, but will those lenses still be tinted by the time they fight their way out of the amazon rain forest.